Dear Reader,

Great news—in February 2013 Harlequin Presents Extra is merging with Presents so you will now be able to find more of your favorite authors in one place as Presents increases from six books a month to eight.

There will be more of the themes you love, such as secret babies, marriages of convenience, scandalous affairs, all with exciting international settings and delicious alpha heroes.

You can also find some of the authors you have come to know and love from Presents Extra in our new contemporary series Harlequin KISS which is launching in February 2013.

So remember, from February onward there will be eight new Presents books available each month!

Happy reading!

The Presents Editors

P.S. Also available this month:

#229 SECRETS OF CASTILLO DEL ARCO
Bound by his Ring
Trish Morey

#230 MARRIAGE BEHIND THE FAÇADE
Bound by his Ring
Lynn Raye Harris

#231 KEEPING HER UP ALL NIGHT
Temptation on her Doorstep
Anna Cleary

#232 THE DEVIL AND THE DEEP
Temptation on her Doorstep
Amy Andrews

"You can't go a day without trying to hook up."

"I think you're exaggerating a little."

Stella stopped pacing and glared at him. "In thirty-six hours, you have flirted with every woman who has crossed your path. And when we get on that boat tomorrow after about twelve hours you're going to start in on me *because you can't help yourself*," she finished a little shrilly.

"You think I can't go a few weeks without flirting with a woman?"

"I dare you. I dare you to go through this whole voyage without flirting with a single woman you meet along the way."

Rick grinned, his gaze locking with hers. "And what do I get?" he asked, his voice low.

The timbre of his voice stroked along all her tired nerve endings as he stared at her with his Vasco eyes.

Stella swallowed. "Get?"

Rick held her gaze. "If I win? How about that kiss that we didn't quite get round to?"

Stella blinked as the bad-boy looked back at her. It was a tantalizing offer. One she knew he didn't expect her to take. But she'd never been one to back down from a dare, and frankly, the idea was as thrilling as it was illicit.

THE DEVIL
AND THE DEEP

AMY ANDREWS

~ Temptation on her Doorstep ~

HARLEQUIN®

entertain, enrich, inspire™

Recycling programs
for this product may
not exist in your area.

ISBN-13: 978-0-373-52900-1

THE DEVIL AND THE DEEP

FIRST NORTH AMERICAN PUBLICATION 2013

Copyright © 2012 by Amy Andrews

Printed in U.S.A.

AMY ANDREWS has always loved writing, and still can't quite believe that she gets to do it for a living. Creating wonderful heroines and gorgeous heroes and telling their stories is an amazing way to pass the day. Sometimes they don't always act as she'd like them to—but then neither do her kids, so she's kind of used to it. Amy lives in the very beautiful Samford Valley, with her husband and aforementioned children, along with six brown chooks and two black dogs.

She loves to hear from her readers. Drop her a line at www.amyandrews.com.au.

Other titles by Amy Andrews available in ebook:

Harlequin Presents®

If you'd like to see more of this author's fantastic books, check out her Harlequin® Medical™ Romances.

For Halle Anne Baxter.
Much loved.

PROLOGUE

*Lady Mary Bingham had never seen such a fine speci-
men of manhood in all her twenty years as she held out
her hand to her unlikely saviour so he could aid her
aboard. Pirate or not, Vasco Ramirez's potent masculinity tingled through every cell of her body. And even had
it not, his piercing blue eyes, the exact colour of warm,
tropical waters that fringed the reefs he was rumoured
to know like the back of his hand, touched a place inside her that she'd never known existed.*

A place she could never now deny.

*She supposed, if she were given to swooning, this
would be as good a time as any. But she wasn't. In fact
she'd always found the practice rather tiresome and
refused to even allow her knees the slightest tremble.
Women who had fits of the vapours and cried for their
smelling salts every two seconds—like her aunt—were
not the kind of women she admired.*

*Her breath hitched as sable lashes framing those in-
credible eyes swept downwards in a frank inspection of
every inch of her body. When his gaze returned to her
face she was left in no doubt that he'd liked what he'd
seen. His thumb lightly stroked the skin of her forearm
and she felt the caress deep inside that newly awak-
ened place.*

Looking at the bronzed angles of his exotic face, she

*knew she should be afraid for had she not just gone from
the frying pan straight into the fire?*

Yet strangely she wasn't.

*Not even when his gaze dropped to the pulse beating rapidly against the milky white skin of her neck. Or
lower to where her breasts strained against the constrictive fabric of her bodice. His lazy inspection of the
agitated rise of her bosom did not elicit fear even when
what it did elicit was reason for fear itself.*

*Her uncle, the bishop, would have declared him an
instrument of the devil. A man willing to lead unsuspecting ladies to the edge of sin but strangely she'd never
felt so compelled to transgress. The thought was titillating and she sucked in a breath, annoyed that this buccaneer had caused such consternation after such short
acquaintance.*

After all, was not one pirate just like the next?

*Mary looked down at the insolent drift of his thumb.
'You will unhand me immediately,' she intoned in a voice
that brooked no argument.*

Ramirez's smile was nine parts charm one part insolence as he slowly—very slowly—ceased the involuntary caress.

*'As you wish,' he murmured, bowing slightly over her
hand, his fingers tracing down the delicate blue veins
of her forearm, whispering over the fragile bones of
her wrist and the flat of her palm as he released her.*

*Lady Mary swallowed as the accented English slid
velvet gloves over already sensitised skin. 'I insist that
you return me to my uncle forthwith.'*

*Vasco admired her pluck. The girl, who he knew to be
barely out of her teens, may well be staring him straight
in the eye but he could smell her fear as only a veteran
of a hundred raids on the high seas could.*

Lord alone knew what had happened to her in the two

days she'd been at the mercy of Juan Del Toro and his ruffians. But something told him this pampered English miss could certainly hold her own.

And virgins fetched a much higher price at the slave markets.

'As you wish,' he murmured again.

Mary narrowed her eyes, suspicious of his easy capitulation. 'You know my uncle? You know who I am?'

He smiled at her. 'You are Lady Mary Bingham. The bishop commissioned me to...retrieve you.'

For the first time in two days Mary could see an end to the nightmare that had begun with her abduction down by the wharfs a mere forty-eight hours before and she almost sagged to the damp floorboards at his feet. She'd heard her former captives talking about slave markets and had been scared witless.

Alas, falling at the feet of a pirate, whether sanctioned by her uncle or not, wasn't something a young woman of good breeding did. 'Thank you,' she said politely. 'I am most grateful for your speedy response. Juan Del Toro's men do not know how to treat a lady.'

'Do not thank me yet, Lady Bingham.' He smiled with steel in his lips. 'There are a lot of miles between here and Plymouth and by the end of it my *men may well care less about you being a lady and more about you being a woman.'*

Mary raised a haughty eyebrow, hoping it disguised the sudden leap in her pulse. 'And you would allow such fiendish behaviour amongst your crew?'

Vasco smiled his most charming smile, his dark tousled hair giving him the look of the devil. 'Amongst my crew? Of course not, Lady Bingham. But captains do enjoy certain privileges...'

STELLA MILLS sighed as she closed down the document on her desktop and dragged herself back from the swashbuckling seventeen hundreds to the reality of the here and now. She could re-read the words that had flowed effortlessly out of her last year and made her an 'overnight' sensation until the cows came home but it didn't change the facts—one book did not a writer make.

One book did not a career make.

No matter how many publishing houses had bid for *Pleasure Hunt* at auction, no matter how many best-seller lists it had made or how many fan letters she'd received or how much money competing film companies had thrown at her for the film rights.

No matter how crazy the romance world had gone for Vasco Ramirez.

They wanted more.

And so did the publisher.

Stella stared at the blinking cursor on the blank page in front of her. The same blinking cursor she'd been staring at for almost a year now.

Oh, God. 'I'm a one-hit wonder,' she groaned as her head hit the keyboard.

A knock on the door interrupted her pity party and she glanced up. Several lines of gobbledygook stared back at her as the knock came again. She grimaced—it seemed she was destined to write nothing but incomprehensible garbage for ever more.

Another knock, more insistent than the last, demanded her attention. 'Coming,' she called as she did what she'd done every day for the past year—deleted the lot.

She hurried to the door and was reaching for the knob as a fourth knock landed. 'Okay, okay, hold your horses,' she said as she wrenched the damn thing open.

Piercing blue eyes, the exact colour of warm, tropical waters that fringed the reefs she knew he knew like the back of his hand, greeted her. She blinked. 'Rick?'

'Stel,' he murmured, leaning forward to kiss first one cheek then the other, inhaling the familiar coconut essence of her.

She shut her eyes briefly as the smell of sea breezes and ocean salt infused her senses the way they always did whenever Riccardo Granville was close. When she opened them again Rick had withdrawn and her mother came into focus, hovering behind his shoulder. Her eyes were rimmed with red and she was biting on her bottom lip.

Her mother lived in London and Rick called the ocean his home. Why were they here? In Cornwall. Together?

Stella frowned as a feeling of doom descended.

'What's wrong?' she asked, looking from one to the other as her pulse wooshed like a raging torrent through her ears.

Her mother stepped forward and hugged her. 'Darling,' she murmured, 'it's Nathan.'

Stella blinked. Her father?

She looked over her mother's shoulder at Rick, his face grim. 'Rick?' she asked, searching for a spark of something—anything—that would bring her back from the precipice she was balanced upon.

Rick looked down at the woman he'd known almost all his thirty years and sadly shook his head. 'I'm sorry.'

CHAPTER ONE

Six months later...

THE cursor still blinked at her from the same blank page. Although Stella rather fancied that it had given up blinking and had moved on to mocking.

There were no words. No story.

No characters spoke in her head. No plot played like a movie reel. No shards of glittering dialogue burnt brightly on her inward eye desperate for release.

There was just the same old silence.

And now grief to boot.

And Diana would be arriving soon.

As if she'd willed it, a knock on the door heralded Stella's closest friend. Normally she'd have leapt from her seat to welcome Diana but not today. In fact, for a moment, she seriously considered not opening the door at all.

Today, Diana was not here as her friend.

Today, Diana was here as a representative from the publisher.

And she'd promised her chapter one...

'I know you're in there. Don't make me break this sucker down.'

The voice was muffled but determined and Stella resigned herself to her fate as she crossed from her work area in the window alcove, with its spectacular one-eighty-degree views of rugged Cornish coastline, to the front door. She drew in a steadying breath as she unlatched it and pulled it open.

Diana opened her arms. 'Babe,' she muttered as she swept Stella into a rib-cracking hug. 'How are you doing? I've been so worried about you.'

Stella settled into the sweet sisterhood of the embrace, suddenly so glad to see her friend she could feel tears prick at the backs of her eyes. They'd only known each other a handful of years since meeting at uni, but Diana had called most nights since the funeral and this was her tenth visit.

'Pretty rubbish,' she admitted into Diana's shoulder.

'Of course you are,' Diana soothed, rubbing her friend's back. 'Your dad died—it comes with the territory.'

Diana's parents had passed away not long before they'd become friends so Stella knew that Diana had intimate acquaintance with grief.

'I want to stop feeling like this.'

Diana hugged her harder. 'You will. Eventually you will. In the meantime you need to do what you need to do. And I think that starts with a nice glass of red.'

Diana held up a bottle of shiraz she'd bought at an off-licence in Penzance on her way to the windswept, cliff-top cottage her friend had taken out a long-term lease on after her strait-laced fiancé, Dreary Dale, hadn't been able to handle the success of *Pleasure Hunt* and had scuttled away with a stick jammed up his butt.

Sure, Stella had insisted her reasons had more to do with the historic coastline's rich pirate history stimulating her muse but, given that no book was forthcoming, Diana wasn't buying it.

Stella looked at her watch and laughed for the first time today. It was two in the afternoon. 'It's a bit early, isn't it?'

Diana tutted her disapproval. 'The sun's up over the yard-arm—isn't that what you nautical types say? Besides, it's November—it's practically night time.'

Diana didn't wait for an answer, dragging her pull-along case inside the house and kicking the door shut with her four-inch-booted heel. She shrugged out of her calf-length, figure-hugging leather coat and unwound her Louis Vuitton scarf from her neck—all without letting go of the bottle. She wore charcoal trousers and a soft pink cashmere sweater, which matched the thick brunette curls that fell against its pearlescent perfection.

Diana was *very* London.

Stella looked down at her own attire and felt like a total slob. Grey sweats, coffee-stained hoodie and fluffy slippers. A haphazard ponytail that she'd scraped together this morning hung limply from her head in an even bigger state of disarray.

Stella was *very* reclusive writer.

Which would be much more romantic if she'd actually bloody written anything in the last eighteen months.

'Sit,' Diana ordered, tinkling her fingers at her friend as she headed towards the cupboard where she knew, from many a drinking session, the wine glasses were housed.

Stella sat on her red leather sofa if, for nothing else, to feel less diminutive. Diana was almost six feet and big boned in a sexy Amazonian, Wonder Woman kind of way. She, on the other hand, was just a couple of centimetres over five feet, fair and round.

'Here,' Diana said, thrusting a huge glass of red at her and clinking the rims together before claiming the bucket chair opposite. 'To feeling better,' she said, then took a decent swig.

'I'll drink to that,' Stella agreed, taking a more measured sip. She stared into the depths of her wine, finding it easier than looking at her friend.

'You don't have the chapter, do you?' Diana asked after the silence had stretched long enough.

Stella looked at Diana over the rim of her glass. 'No,' she murmured. 'I'm sorry.'

Diana nodded. 'It's okay.'

Stella shook her head and uttered what had been on her mind since the writer's block had descended all those months ago. 'What if I only ever have one book in me?'

The fear had gnawed away at her since finishing the first book. Dale's desertion had added to it. Her father's death had cemented it.

Vasco Ramirez had demanded to be written. He'd strutted straight out of her head onto the page in all his swashbuckling glory. He had been a joy, his story a gift that had flowed effortlessly.

And now?

Now they wanted another pirate and she had nothing.

Diana held up a hand, waving the question away. 'You don't,' she said emphatically.

'But what if I do?'

Stella had never known the sting of rejection and the mere thought was paralysing. What if Joy, her editor, hated what she wrote? What if she laughed?

She'd had a dream ride—from a six-figure auction with a multi-book contract to *New York Times* best-seller to a movie deal.

What if it had all been a fluke?

Diana stabbed her finger at the air in her general direction. 'You. Don't.'

Stella felt a surge of guilt mix with the shiraz in her veins, giving it an extra charge. Diana had championed her crazy foray into writing from the beginning, encouraging her to take a break from being an English teacher and write the damn book.

She'd been the first to read it. The first to know its potential, insisting that she take it to show her boss, who was looking for exactly what Stella had written—a meaty historical romance. As an editorial assistant in a London publishing house Diana had been adamant it was a blockbuster and

Stella had been flabbergasted when Diana's prediction of a quick offer had come to pass.

She smiled at her friend, hoping it didn't come across as desperate on the outside as it felt on the inside. 'Will you get sacked if you return to London empty-handed?'

Almost a year past Stella's deadline, Joy had pulled out the big guns to get her recalcitrant star to deliver. She knew how close Diana and Stella were so she'd sent Diana to do whatever it took to get book number two.

Diana shook her head. 'No. We're not going to talk about this tonight. Tonight, we get messy drunk, tomorrow we talk about the book. Deal?'

Stella felt the knot in her shoulder muscles release like an elastic band and she smiled. 'Deal.'

Two hours later, a storm had drawn night in a little earlier than usual. Wind howled around the house, lashing at the shutters, not that the two women cosied up by the fire were aware. They were on their second bottle of wine and almost at the bottom of a large packet of crisps and were laughing hysterically about their uni days.

A sharp rap at the door caused them both to startle then burst out laughing at their comic-book reactions.

'Bloody hell.' Diana clutched her chest. 'I think I just had a heart attack.'

Stella laughed as she rose a little unsteadily. 'Impossible, red wine's supposed to be good for the heart.'

'Not in these quantities it's not,' Diana said and Stella cracked up again as she headed towards the door.

'Wait, where are you going?' Diana muttered as she also clambered to her feet.

Stella frowned. 'To open the door.'

'But what if it's a two-headed moor monster?' Even through her wine goggles Diana could see the rain lashing the window pane behind Stella's desk. 'It is the very definition of a dark and stormy night out there, babe.'

Stella hiccupped. 'Well, I don't think they knock but I'll politely tell it to shoo and point out that Bodmin is a little north of here.'

Diana cracked up and Stella was still chuckling as she opened the door.

To Vasco Ramirez. In the flesh.

Light from inside the cottage bathed the bronzed angles of his jaw and cheekbones, fell softly against his mouth and illuminated his blue eyes to tourist-brochure perfection. His shoulder-length hair, a relic from his tearaway teens, hung in damp strips around his face and water droplets clung to those incredible sable lashes.

He looked every inch the pirate.

'Rick?' Her breath stuttered to a halt as it always did when he was too close, sucking up all her oxygen. The recalcitrant memory of an almost-kiss over a decade ago flitted like a butterfly through her grey matter.

Rick smiled down at a frowning Stella. 'Now what sort of greeting is that?' he teased as he moved in for his standard double cheek kiss.

Coconut embraced him. Nathan had bought Stella coconut body products every year for her birthday and she'd faithfully worn them. Still was, apparently.

Stella shut her eyes and waited for the choirs of angels in her head to start singing *hallelujah* as the aroma of salt and sea enveloped her. He was, after all, so perfect he had to be heaven-sent.

She blinked as he pulled away. 'Is everything okay?' she asked.

Her heart beat a little faster in her chest. Which had nothing to do with the erotic scrape of his perpetual three-day growth or the brief brush of his lips, and everything to do with his last visit.

Rick didn't just drop by.

Last time he'd arrived unannounced on her doorstep looking bleaker than the North Sea in winter, the news had not been good.

'Is Mum—?'

Rick pressed his fingers against her mouth, hushing her. 'Linda's fine, Stel. Everything's fine.'

She almost sagged against him in relief. Certainly her mouth did. He smiled at her as he withdrew his hand and she smiled back, and with the wind whipping around them and flurries of raindrops speckling their skin it was as if they were kids again, standing on the bow of the *Persephone* as a storm chased them back into harbour.

'So…not a monster from the moors, then?' Diana asked, interrupting their shared reverie.

Rick looked over Stella's shoulder straight into the eyes of a vaguely familiar, striking brunette. She looked at him with frank admiration and he grinned.

God, but he loved women.

Particularly women like this. The kind that liked to laugh and have a good time, enjoyed a flirt and some no-strings company.

'Honey, I can be whatever you want me to be,' he said, pushing off the door jamb, brushing past Stella and extending his hand. 'Hi. Rick. I think we've already met?'

Diana smiled as she shook his hand. 'Yes. When you were here for the funeral. Diana,' she supplied.

'Ah, yes, that's right,' Rick said, stalling a little. He'd been so caught up in his shock and disbelief and being strong for Stella and Linda that he'd not really taken anything in. 'You work for Stel's publishers?'

Diana grinned, her eyes twinkling, not remotely insulted that Rick had struggled to remember her. 'Took you a while.'

Stella watched her bestie and her…whatever the hell Rick was—old family friend? deceased father's business partner?

substitute brother?—flirt effortlessly. Now why couldn't she be more like that? The only time she'd been comfortable, truly comfortable, with a man had been with a fictional pirate.

Even her relationship with Dale had been lukewarm by comparison.

A blast of rain spattered against her neck, bringing her out of her state of bewilderment, and she realised she still had the door wide open. She shook her head at her absent-mindedness.

'To what do we owe the pleasure?' she asked, shutting the weather out and joining the chatty twosome in the centre of the room.

Rick looked down at Stella's cute little button nose. 'Well—' he winked at her before returning his attention to Diana and running his finger around the rim of her glass '—I heard a whisper there was a party going on.'

Diana laughed. She looked at Stella. 'You never told me he had ESP.' Then she scurried to the kitchen to get another glass.

Rick watched her for a moment before returning his gaze to Stella. She stared up at him and the familiar feeling of wanting to wrap her up swelled in his chest. 'How are you doing, Stel?' he murmured.

Rick had felt the loss of Nathan Mills probably even more profoundly than his own father. Nathan had been his guardian and mentor since Anthony Granville had got himself killed in a bar fight when Rick had been seven. The man had been the closest thing to a father he had, had curbed all his hot-headed brashness and he felt his loss in a hundred different ways every day.

He could only imagine how Stella must feel.

Stella shrugged, feeling again the mutual despair that had added an extra depth to their bond. She fell into the empathy that shone in his luminescent gaze. Sometimes it was hard to reconcile the impulsive, teenage bad-boy of her fantasies with the hardworking, responsible, compassionate man in front of her.

'I hate it,' she whispered.

The truth was Stella hadn't seen her father regularly since she'd started university and joined the workforce.

Become a grown-up, as her mother would say.

A flying visit at Christmas, the arrival in the mail of a single perfect shell he'd found on a beach somewhere that always made her smile, an occasional email with pictures of him and Rick and some amazing find at the bottom of a sea bed.

But just knowing he was out there doing what he loved, following his wild boyhood dreams of sunken galleons, had kept her whole world in balance.

And now he was gone, nothing was the same.

'I know,' he murmured, putting his arm around her shoulder and pulling her into his chest. 'I hate it too.'

And he did. He hated doing what he did without the one person who truly understood *why* by his side. He hated turning to tell Nathan something and him not being there. He hated the absence of wise words and Nathan's particular brand of bawdy humour around the dinner table.

Rick shut his eyes against the loss he still felt so acutely and sank into her, enjoying the familiarity of having her close. He liked how she tucked into him just right. How her head fitted perfectly under his chin and how his chest was just the right height to pillow her cheek and how she always smelled liked coconut.

As kids he'd been the pirate and she'd been the mermaid and they'd played endless games revolving around sunken treasure. Not very politically correct these days, he supposed, but they'd amused themselves for countless hours and forged a bond that he still felt today.

Of course there'd been times, during their teenage years, when their games had taken a certain risqué turn and while they'd never indulged, they'd diced pretty close.

Holding her like this reminded him just how close.

'Okay, okay, you two,' Diana teased, pushing a glass of red

wine into Rick's hand. 'No maudlin tonight. That's the rule. Eat, drink and be merry tonight.'

Rick forced himself to step away, grateful that Diana was here to ground them in the present. He'd thought a lot about Stella since Nathan had died, more than usual.

And not all of those thoughts had been pure.

He accepted the wine. 'Good plan,' he said, clinking glasses with them both.

Stella indicated the lounge chairs huddled around the fireplace and watched as Rick shrugged out of his navy duffle coat to reveal well-worn jeans that clung in all the right places and a thick turtle-neck, cable-knit sweater.

Even off the boat the man looked as if he belonged at sea.

Diana lounged back against the cushions, inspecting him dispassionately, her wine goggles making the job a little difficult. She pointed at him over the rim of her glass.

'There's something familiar about you,' she slurred.

Stella didn't like the look of speculation on her friend's face. She'd seen that dogged look before and didn't want to give Diana too much latitude.

'Yes, you met him at the funeral,' she said, hopefully redirecting her friend's thoughts that tended to fancy after several glasses of red.

Diana narrowed her eyes. 'Nope,' she said as she shook her head. 'I have this feeling I know you beyond that.' Even at the funeral all suited and polished he'd looked vaguely familiar to her but now, looking all lone-wolf-of-the-sea, there was definitely something she recognised about him.

Was it his eyes? Or maybe his hair?

Rick chuckled. 'Maybe I look like your great uncle Cyril?'

Diana burst out laughing as she sipped on her drink and Stella even envied her that. She had a jingly laugh that sounded like Tinkerbell waving her magic wand. Stella had no doubt that red wine would be pouring out of her nose had she tried that same manoeuvre.

Diana wagged her finger. 'Good try but *you* don't look like *anyone's* great uncle Cyril.' She narrowed her eyes again and nudged the side of her nose three times with her index finger. 'Don't you worry. I *will* remember. I may just need—' she looked at her almost empty wine glass '—a while.'

Rick saluted. 'I look forward to the final outcome.'

Diana nodded. 'As well you should.'

Rick looked over at Stella sitting quietly watching the byplay. The firelight spun the escaping tendrils of her long blonde hair into golden streams and he was once again reminded of their childhood games when she'd been the mermaid singing his ship onto the rocks. How many times had he snorkelled over reefs with her, her long blonde hair flowing behind her just like the mermaids from ancient mythology?

'So,' he said when the silence had stretched enough. 'Did you get it?'

Stella frowned at him. 'Get what?'

'Your half.'

'My half of what?'

Rick grinned. 'The map?'

Stella shook her head. 'What on earth are you talking about?' she asked.

Rick's eyebrows drew together in a frown to match hers as he placed his half-empty glass on the coffee table. 'You should have received it early last week. I posted it ages ago.'

Diana rolled her eyes. 'She probably has. She's just not been responding to any correspondence.'

Stella blushed at her friend's astuteness as Diana made her way to the hall stand. Unopened mail oozed all over the edges of the sturdy eighteenth-century oak and Stella felt her cheeks grow warmer. She'd been avoiding any attempt at communication with the outside world—particularly from her editor. She didn't open her mail unless it had a window. She screened all her calls. She didn't go to her inbox.

Diana quickly riffled through the mound of mail, letters

and other miscellaneous items that had made it through Stella's front door, some of it spilling haphazardly to the floor. She pulled out a large flat yellow envelope with enough stamps to start a collection.

'This it?' she asked holding it up.

Rick nodded. 'Arrr,' he said in his best pirate accent. 'That be it.'

It was Stella's turn to roll her eyes. Rick had perfected the pirate vernacular as a child, lending an authenticity to their imaginary games.

Diana laughed as she rejoined them, thrusting the envelope at Stella. 'Ooh, you speak pirate?'

Rick grinned. 'Aye, my lovely.'

'Forget it,' Stella murmured absently as she turned the envelope over and over in her hands. There was a variety of colourful postal stamps and airmail stickers adorning the front. 'Diana's a Jack Sparrow fan. You're wasting your time.'

Rick look affronted. 'Are you saying I'm not Captain Jack material?'

It was on the tip of Stella's tongue to say that he was a thousand times sexier than the iconic film character. He was broader and taller with better oral hygiene and more scruples.

'Hmm, I don't know,' Diana mused. 'I'm sure a little more scruffed up...'

But Stella wasn't listening. Her father's distinctive handwriting had drawn her gaze and she touched the letters with great reverence as if they could somehow bring him back.

Rick glanced at Diana as Stella's continuing silence fell loudly around them. She shrugged at him hopelessly and he could tell that Stella's grief touched her too.

'Where did you get this?' Stella asked.

'I finally got around to cleaning out Nathan's desk. It was in a drawer. There was one for me as well.'

Stella nodded absently at his response. It was strange receiving something from her father six months after his death. Like a hand extending from the grave.

'Aren't you going to open it?' he asked quietly.

Stella looked up at him through the blonde stripes of her half-up-half-down fringe. 'Do I want to?'

He grinned and nodded. 'If it's what I think it is you do. You really do.'

Stella doubted it but she turned the envelope over and neatly sliced open the back. A sheath of loose papers lay within and she pulled them out after another encouraging nod from Rick. A brief note from her father was paper-clipped to the front.

Stel,
Inigo's treasure is there, I just know it.
You and Rick go find it.
Make me proud.
Daddy.

Stella swallowed hard and for a moment the bold vertical slashes blurred in front of her eyes. Finding out on autopsy that her father had been riddled with cancer and wondering if the scuba-diving *accident* had really been an accident had been hard to come to terms with.

But this seemed to confirm that he'd known his days were numbered and chosen to go in his own way doing what he'd loved most.

She glanced at Rick. 'You got the same?'

He nodded and she looked back at the documents, leafing through the rest. A hand-drawn map was at the very back.

Or half a map to be precise.

'What's this?' she asked, not quite comprehending her father's frenetic squiggles around the margins.

'The other half of this,' Rick said, pulling out a folded page from his back pocket, unfolding it and laying it on the coffee table.

Diana sat forward. 'Is that a…treasure map?'

Rick grinned. 'Sort of. It shows the potential resting places of Captain Inigo Alvarez's ship, *La Sirena*.'

Diana scrunched up her face, trying to remember her schoolgirl Spanish. 'The…?'

'The Mermaid,' Stella supplied.

'Oh my,' Diana said. 'How exciting! Inigo Alvarez…' She rolled the name around her tongue. 'He sounds positively dishy.'

Rick laughed. 'He was. A late-eighteenth-century pirate known as the Robin Hood of the seven seas. Robbing the rich to give to the poor.'

Stella blasted Rick with a *down-boy* glare. 'Robin Hood of the high seas,' she tisked, shaking her head in disgust. 'That's all just anecdotal and you know it. Do not encourage her.'

'Drat,' Diana mused.

'Okay, maybe he was as bloodthirsty and marauding as the rest of them but there's heaps of historical documents citing his and *The Mermaid*'s existence,' he said calmly. 'You used to believe,' Rick reminded her.

They both had. Everyone in the salvaging industry seemed to have a story about the mysterious Captain Alvarez and as children they'd listened to each one until he'd grown large in both their imaginations. Rick picked up the papers that had accompanied the map, the same ones that had been in his envelope. Years of Nathan's research into a character that had captured them both.

'What happened to him?' Diana asked.

Rick looked at a captivated Diana. 'He just disappeared off the face of the earth. There were rumours at the time that *The Mermaid* went down laden with stolen booty during a vicious storm.'

'Where?' Diana whispered, sucked in even if Stella was sitting back in her chair, refusing to be drawn. 'Here somewhere, right?' she asked, picking up Stella's half of the map and joining the two pieces together on the coffee table.

Rick shook his head. 'Nathan obviously thought so. He's drawn this up from his research over the years so I guess it would be hard to be sure. But he was the best damn intuitive treasure hunter I've ever known and if he thinks Inigo's ship is here somewhere, then I'm willing to bet it is too.'

'So why didn't he go after it himself?' Stella demanded, getting up off the chair and heading for the kitchen sink. When she got there she tipped out her almost-full glass of wine. She was suddenly angry with her father.

If he'd known he was dying, why hadn't he told her? Why hadn't he got treatment? Why hadn't he come home?

'When did he have the time, Stel, with so many other projects—sure things—on the books?'

Stella looked up at the reproach in his voice, feeling suddenly guilty. They'd both known Nathan's plans had always involved finding Inigo's treasure...one day...when he retired...

'Why on earth did he give us half a map each? He must have known I was just going to give you my half and let you have at it.'

She'd loved her father and he had given her a magical childhood filled with sunken treasure and tropical waters but it had been a long time since she'd been a little girl who believed in pirates and mermaids. And the romance of that world had always warred with the realities of her life—divorced parents, divided loyalties.

Rick stood and walked towards her. He could tell she was struggling with the same emotions he had when he'd seen Nathan's handwriting again and the memories it had stirred.

'I think he knew his time was drawing to a close and maybe it was his way to keep us connected? I think he wanted us to go and do this together and I think it would be a great way to honour his memory. What do you say? The long-range weather forecast is good. You want to come on a treasure hunt with me?'

Stella glared at Rick as his not-so-subtle guilt trip found its mark. Well, it wouldn't work. 'Are you crazy? I can't go gallivanting around the bloody ocean. My editor would have apoplexy. My book is way overdue and I have probably the worst case of writer's block in the history of written language, don't I, Diana?'

She looked at her friend for confirmation, who did so with a vigorous nod of her head.

'Well, this is exactly what you need.' He grinned, unperturbed. 'Nothing like the open ocean to stimulate the muse.'

Stella stared at him askance. 'Don't you have other salvage jobs on the go?'

Rick shrugged. 'Nothing the guys can't handle. Besides, it won't be a salvage job, just a recon mission, see what we can find. A few weeks, four at the most. Just you and me and the open ocean. Salt, sea air and sunshine. You could get a tan,' he cajoled as he took in her pallor. 'It'll be just like we were kids again.'

Stella shook her head against the temptation and romance of yesteryear, which appealed to her on a primal level she didn't really understand. She dragged her gaze away from his seductive mouth.

They weren't kids any more.

'I can't. I have a book to write.'

'Come on,' he murmured, feeling the longing inside her even if she couldn't. 'You know you want to. You always wrote like crazy whenever you were on the *Persephone*. Remember? You were always scribbling away in that writing pad.'

She remembered. She'd either had her head stuck in a book or she'd been writing something. He'd teased her about it mercilessly. She should have known back then she was destined to be a writer. 'I can't. Can I, Diana?'

Diana looked at Stella. Then at Rick. Then back at her

friend. If anyone needed a change of scenery it was Stella. These four walls were obviously becoming a prison for her despite the view—maybe mixing it up a little would get the juices flowing again.

And if the open ocean was where she was most creative…

Joy would have a fit but Diana had a hunch that this was just what her friend needed. She bloody hoped so because her head would be on the chopping block if Stella returned tanned and still bookless.

She stood and joined them in the kitchen. 'I think you should go. I think it's a great idea.'

Stella blinked. 'What?' she said as Rick's grin trebled.

'*This*,' he said, slipping his arm around Diana's shoulders, 'is a wise woman.'

'Thank you.' Diana beamed at him.

'Come on, Stel. *I dare you.*'

Stella rolled her eyes. As kids their relationship had thrived on dares and one-upmanship, Stella hell-bent on proving she could keep up with a boy.

Dare you to swim through that hole in the wreck. Something expressly forbidden by her father. *Dare you to bring a coin up from the bottom.* Also forbidden. *Dare you to touch that manta ray.* Just plain stupid.

It was a wonder they'd both survived.

She remembered when the dares had stopped. That evening on deck when she'd dared him to kiss her. She wondered if he remembered. His eyes glittered back at her—all bad-boy blue—and she *knew* he remembered.

'Tell you what,' Rick said as he pulled himself back from that ancient memory that still resonated in his dreams, 'don't decide now. Sleep on it first, okay. I bet it won't seem as crazy in the morning.'

Stella was willing to bet that in the cold light of day *and* stone-cold sober it would not only seem crazy, it would actually *be* crazy.

Utterly certifiable.

He leaned forward and kissed her forehead, then winked at Diana. 'Can I crash here?'

Stella felt like a child between two grown-ups. 'What, no girl in this port, sailor?' she asked waspishly. The man had never lacked for company on shore.

Rick chuckled. 'Not one who can make pancakes like you.'

'Ah,' she said, realising she was being churlish and making an effort to get them back to their usual repartee. 'So you only want me for my pancakes.'

'And your half of the map.' He grinned. 'I'm beat. I need a shower. Then I need to sleep for a week. Towels still in the same place?' he asked as he left them, not waiting for an answer.

Diana watched him go. 'Wow.'

Stella nodded. 'Yes.'

She turned to face the sink, leaning her elbows against the cool steel as she looked out of the large bay window into the bleak dark night. Diana joined her, still sipping at her wine.

'Does he wear contacts?' she mused. 'It's quite striking to see a man with such dark colouring have such blue eyes.'

Stella nodded again. She'd been captivated by them for as long as she could remember. 'Yes, it's really quite mesmerising, isn't it?'

'Which room are you in, Diana?'

Both women started guiltily as the voice from behind them had them straightening and whipping around to face Rick. He was naked except for possibly the world's smallest towel around his waist, clutched at the side where it didn't quite meet. His blue eyes looked even bluer with less of anything much to detract from them.

'The one on the left,' Stella confirmed after a quick glance at a gawking, mute-looking Diana.

'Great, I'll doss down in the other.' He smiled at both of them. 'See you in the morning, ladies.'

Stella and Diana watched him as he swaggered away, the towel slipping as he gave up on trying to keep it on. They caught a glimpse of one naked buttock just before he disappeared around the corner.

A buttock adorned with a very sexy, perfectly round, dark brown birthmark, right in the middle of a very sexy dimple.

Diana gasped as suddenly everything fell into place. Bronzed colouring, piercing blue eyes, long shaggy hair, a mouth made for sin and a very cute blemish in a very specific place.

'Oh, my God!' She looked at Stella. 'That's why he's so familiar. It's him—he's Vasco Ramirez!'

CHAPTER TWO

STELLA blushed furiously. 'Shh,' she hissed. 'Don't be pre-posterous.'

Diana laughed. 'Methinks the lady doth protest too much.'

Stella turned back to the sink, busying herself with wash-ing out her wine glass. 'There are some similarities…' she admitted.

'Similarities?' Diana hooted. 'I *knew* I knew him…I just couldn't figure out where from. I mean, hell, let's face it, if I'd met him somewhere before I'd hardly be likely to for-get him—the man's a total hottie. And, I have to say—' she nudged Stella '—looks like a total sex fiend.'

'Diana!'

She shrugged. 'In a good way.'

'Well, don't look at me,' Stella muttered. 'You know I've only ever been with Dale.'

Diana tisked. 'I can't believe you've never gone there… well, I mean you've obviously thought about it because you wrote an entire three-hundred-and-seventy-five page sexual fantasy about the man—'

'*I did not,*' Stella denied, picking up a tea towel and briskly drying the glass.

Diana crooked an eyebrow at her. 'Stella, this is me. Diana. Who knows you.'

Stella looked into her friend's eyes and could see that she

knew the truth. She sagged against the sink. 'Okay, yes,' she sighed. 'Rick was the inspiration for Vasco.'

Stella hadn't set out to write a book with Rick as the hero but Vasco had taken on Rick's features in a totally organic way. She hadn't even been truly aware of it until she'd written the first kiss.

And then it had been so blindingly obvious she'd wondered why it had taken her so long.

'Hah! I knew it!' Diana clapped delightedly.

Stella rolled her eyes. 'This is between you and me, Diana,' she said, placing a hand on her friend's arm. 'Promise?'

'Don't worry,' Diana said, waving a dismissive hand, 'your secret is safe with me.'

'Thank you,' Stella said, releasing a breath as she shuffled away from the sink and headed towards the fire.

'Well, there's only one thing for it now,' Diana said as she followed Stella and plonked herself down on one of the lounge chairs. 'You have to go with him.'

Stella looked up from her log poking. 'What?'

'The man obviously inspires you to write. You need inspiration. *You need to write.* Problem solved.'

'Joy doesn't want another Vasco Ramirez, Diana.'

'Yes, she does,' Diana said. 'That's exactly what she wants. Vasco sold like hot cakes. Vasco is king. Of course she wants you to do another Vasco.'

Stella gave her friend an impatient look. 'You know what I mean.'

Diana sighed. She didn't want to pull out the big guns. 'Babe, things are going to start to get nasty. And trust me, you don't want to be with a publishing house that plays hard ball. There'll be lawyers. It's time to quit the whole writer's block nonsense and write.'

Stella felt Diana's words slice into her side. 'You think it's nonsense—that I'm making it up?'

Diana shook her head. She knew Stella's instant fame had

compounded her already entrenched second-book syndrome and her father's death had just aggravated everything further. She totally got that Stella's muse had deserted her. But…

'The lawyers will think it is, babe.'

'I just need a little more time,' Stella muttered.

Diana nodded. 'And you should take it. Absolutely. Go with Rick, get inspired. Come back replenished.'

Stella glanced at her friend. She made it sound so easy. She shook her head. 'It's crazy.'

'Why?' Diana challenged. 'Because you have a thing for him?'

'I do not have a thing for him,' Stella denied quickly. A little too quickly perhaps. 'He's an old, *old* friend,' she clarified, not bothering to keep the exasperation out of her voice. 'We've known each other *for ever.* There is no *thing.*'

Diana looked at her friend. Oh, there so *was* a thing.

Even better.

Lord alone knew, if she hadn't had sex for almost a year on top of fairly pedestrian sex for the previous five she'd be looking at a way of fixing that pronto. And if it so happened that the man of Stella's fantasies was there at the precise moment she decided to break the drought, then surely everyone won?

'So it shouldn't be a problem, then?' Diana asked innocently. She held up her hand as Stella went to speak again. 'Look, Rick's right. Just sleep on it. I know it's a lot to consider but, for what it's worth, I think you're mad if you don't.'

'But the book…' Stella murmured in a last-ditch effort to make Diana see sense.

Diana shrugged. 'Whatever you're doing here on good old terra firma ain't working, is it, babe?'

Stella went to bed determined to wake up in the morning and tell both Rick and Diana to go to hell.

But that was before the dream.

She dreamt all night of a mermaid following a pirate ship. No…

She was the mermaid and *she* was following the pirate ship. Inside the hull a lone, rich, tenor voice would occasionally sing a deep mournful song of lost love. It was a thing of beauty and she'd fallen in love with the man even though she'd never laid eyes on him. But she knew he was a prisoner and she knew with an urgency that beat like the swell of the ocean in her breast that she had to save him.

That he was the one for her.

Stella awoke, the last tendrils of the dream still gliding over her skin like the cool kiss of sea water. It was so vivid for a moment she could almost feel the water frothing her hair in a glorious golden crown around her head.

The urge to write thrummed through her veins and she quickly opened the drawer of her bedside table, locating the stash of pens and paper she always kept there. She brushed off the dust and started to scribble and in ten minutes she'd written down the bones of a plot and some detailed description of Lucinda, the mermaid.

When she finished she sat back and stared at the words in front of her. They were a revelation. And not just because she'd written something she didn't have the immediate urge to delete, but because it was a whole new approach.

Stella hadn't imagined for even a minute that the heroine's point of view would take precedence in her head. Vasco had been so strong and dominant, striding onto the page, demanding to be heard, that she'd assumed starting with the hero was always going to be her process.

All this time she'd been beating herself up about not being able to see a hero, getting her knickers in a twist because, no matter how hard she tried to visualise one, no hero was forthcoming.

And he still wasn't. But Lucinda *was* fully formed and she was *awesome*.

Lucinda excited her as nothing had since Vasco had arrived. Lucinda was no Lady Mary waiting around to be saved. The world had gone crazy for Vasco last time, this time they would go crazy for Lucinda.

She could feel it deep inside in the same place that had told her Vasco was special, but she'd been too inexperienced to listen.

Well, she was listening now.

God, Joy was probably going to have a fit at her kick-ass mermaid. She could hear her now saying, *But what about Inigo, Stella?*

Stella gasped as his name came to her. *Inigo*. Of course that was his name. *Inigo*. It had to be Inigo.

It was working.

The buzz was back. *The magic was here.*

Inigo would be strong and noble, a perfect match for Lucinda because a strong woman required a man to equal her. A man secure in himself. A man who would understand the divided loyalties she endured every day and wouldn't demand that she chose between the sea and land.

A subject that Stella could write about intimately.

God, why hadn't she thought to approach her story from this way before? It seemed so obvious now. She kicked off the sheets, reached for her polar fleece dressing gown.

She had to get out of here. Had to get to her computer.

She almost laughed as she tripped over her gown in haste. The revelation had come just in time. It had saved her. There was no time now for seafaring adventures.

There was a mermaid to write. A hero to rescue.

Lucinda was calling.

Inigo too.

Stella padded straight to her computer, notes in hand. She drummed her fingers on the desk as she waited for it to power up. As soon as she was able, she opened a new word document and typed *The Siren's Call* in the header.

She blinked at it. Her fingers hadn't even consulted her brain. The title had just appeared.

It was all happening.

Then the cursor winked at her from a blank page and the buzz and pulse inside shrivelled like a sultana.

What? No...

She took her hands off the keyboard, waited a moment or two, then placed them back on. She waited for her fingers to roam over the keys, pressing randomly to make words on the page. She consulted her notes and desperately tried to recall spunky Lucinda.

But nothing came.

'You're up early,' Rick's voice murmured in her ear as he plonked a steaming hot cup of coffee at her elbow and she almost leapt two feet off the chair.

'Bloody hell, Rick, do you mind?' she griped as she clutched at her chest. Had she been that focused she hadn't even noticed he was up, or smelled the aroma of coffee?

'Whoa there, sorry, didn't mean to startle you.' He grinned. 'What are you working on?'

Stella minimised the document, leaving only her screen saver to view. She glared up at him. Then she wished she hadn't. He was wearing long stripy flannelette pyjama bottoms and nothing on top. The drawstring was pulled low and tight on his hips, revealing way too much skin right at her eye level.

Suddenly Lucinda whispered in her head again, murmuring her story, buzzing through Stella's veins like an illicit drug. Flashes of her childhood felt sweet against Stella's tongue. Lucinda's despair over Inigo tightened Stella's chest.

This was crazy.

Stella turned back to the computer, the need to write an imperative even with Rick hovering. But as suddenly as it had come upon her the flow stopped. Stella blinked—was there a tap somewhere that somebody had just turned off?

Rick let out a long low wolf whistle, ignoring her silence—Stella had never been a morning person. 'Sexy cover,' he murmured, taking the other chair at the desk and straddling it. 'Great rack.'

Stella, still willing Lucinda to come back, took a moment to work out what Rick was referring to. She looked at her computer, the cover for *Pleasure Hunt* her screen saver. Lady Bingham's flowing scarlet dress with the plunging neckline made the best of her assets, pushing her milky breasts practically into the face of the leering Vasco Ramirez.

'Nice.' Stella glared at him as she reopened her blank page, obliterating the screen saver.

Lucinda? Lucinda? Where are you?

'I'm just saying, he seems to be enjoying the view and I can't blame him.'

It would indeed be hypocritical, Rick thought, considering how very much he enjoyed that kind of view himself. The kind of view that Stella was giving him right at this moment as her gown flapped open and the low-cut vest shirt she wore gaped a little to reveal a glimpse of soft female breast.

The view he was trying to ignore.

He'd had a lot of practice at ignoring Stella's breasts, given his treasured honorary position in the Mills family, but that didn't mean it had been easy—then or now. Witness the time he'd lost his head and succumbed to her kissing dare with a heady mix of trepidation, challenge and anticipation.

Anticipation that had been building since the summer she'd arrived on the *Persephone* with curves and a bra.

Being sprung by her father before he'd reached his target and Nathan's little *chat* with him afterwards had set him straight. And he'd never betrayed Nathan's trust.

Not consciously anyway.

'He's practically drooling,' he murmured, gaze firmly fixed on the screen.

Stella turned to Rick to defend Vasco. To say that her hero

was not a salivating pervert, but of course she couldn't because the man *was* a scoundrel of the highest order and she knew damn well he'd appreciated Mary's cleavage as he'd appreciated countless other women's cleavages before he'd met Mary and probably still was, out there in fiction land somewhere.

But it all died on her lips as Lucinda's sweet melodic voice started up a dialogue in her head again, talking about her father disowning her for following a whim and her mother's grief over their rift.

The implications stunk to high heaven.

Oh, God. Please no, not this, Lucinda. I'll do anything, I'll go anywhere else you want, but not this.

Just then Diana entered the room, negating the need for Stella to say anything, for which she was grateful. She yawned loudly and bade them both a good morning as she made her way to the kitchen in her clingy satin Hello Kitty pyjamas and poured herself a coffee from the percolator.

Rick whistled. 'Well, hello Kitty.'

Stella rolled her eyes. Diana grinned as she plonked herself down in a lounge chair.

'So?' she demanded. 'Are you going with Rick or what?'

'Good question, Miss Kitty.' Rick nodded. 'Well?' he asked, seeking Stella's gaze.

Even just looking at him looking at her, Stella could feel the story buzzing through her veins. She could feel Lucinda beckoning her like the siren she was, waving at her from the rocks, drawing her ever closer to her doom.

She looked back at the computer screen with its mocking little cursor and acres of blankness and got nothing.

She sighed as Lucinda won. 'Yes. I'm going.'

'Really?' Rick stood and punched a fist in the air at her curt nod.

How on earth was she going to share a boat with him when she hadn't had sex in ages and he'd always been her private fantasy go-to man?

They were friends.

They were business partners, for crying out loud!

'I've booked us two tickets to Cairns on a flight that leaves Heathrow early this evening.'

'Ooh, cocky, I like that,' Diana murmured, sipping her coffee.

Stella ignored her, as did Rick who, Stella knew from experience, must be biting his tongue to let that one go.

'Australia?' she squeaked.

Rick shrugged. 'The map's Micronesia and I haven't taken the *Dolphin* out since I bought her.'

Stella stood. 'You bought the *Dolphin*?'

Rick had been fascinated with the thirty-foot classic wooden yacht for as long as she could remember. They'd seen it in various ports over the years and it had always been a dream of his to have it for himself.

'When?'

He grinned. 'A few months ago. I finally tracked her down in New Zealand and had her refitted in Cairns. She's ready to go.'

Stella felt a little thrill that had nothing to do with Lucinda. Rick had talked about it so much over the years it had almost become her dream too. 'So we're going to take her?' she clarified.

He nodded. 'If you want to. I could always hire something bigger, whiter, more pretentious if you preferred.'

Stella smiled at the distaste curling his lips. The Mills and Granville salvage fleet was three big white, powerful boats strong and, while she knew Rick was proud of what her father and he had built up, his passion had always been the classic beauty of the *Dolphin*. 'Perish the thought.' She grinned.

Rick grinned back at her and felt a hum of excitement warm his belly. There was something different about Stel this morning. Last night she'd been the Stella he'd always known—slopping around, no airs and graces, no special treatment.

This morning she glowed as if she had a secret that no one else knew. Her olive-green eyes seemed to radiate purpose. Her cheeks seemed pinker. Even her scraped-back ponytail seemed to have more perk in it.

She looked like women did when they were pregnant, as if they were doing something truly amazing and they knew it.

She was *radiant*.

It was quite breathtaking and his stomach clenched inside in a way that, as a man, he was all too familiar with.

But not where she was concerned.

He looked at Diana, all sleepy and tousled with her knowing eyes and cute mouth, and waited for the twinge to come again.

He got nothing.

Hmm.

'Right.' He drained his coffee quickly. There were things to do and not being here for a while was a good option. 'Gotta go get some things sorted. I'll see you both later.'

Stella busied herself in the kitchen until Rick left the house five minutes later. 'How are you going to break it to Joy?' she asked Diana.

'Oh, forget that,' Diana said, waving the query away. 'I'll tell her you've gone off to be inspired. There are much more important things to discuss.'

Stella frowned. 'There are?'

Diana nodded vigorously, her shirt pulling tight across her chest as she leaned over the kitchen bench. 'You two should have sex,' she said.

Stella almost dropped her second mug of coffee. *Was she mad?* 'Ah no.' She shook her head. 'Bad. Idea.'

Diana raised an eyebrow. 'Okay, well, you're going to have to explain that one to me.'

Stella didn't even know where to start with how bad an idea it was. 'Because we're friends. *And* colleagues. I'm his silent partner, for crying out loud! And trust me, I know better than anyone not to get tangled up with a man of the sea. They never choose land. They never choose love.'

Diana rolled her eyes. 'You're just having sex with him, not marrying the man.'

'Which is just as well because men of the sea should not marry. My father chose the sea over my mother. Rick's mother left when he was a baby because his father wouldn't settle on land. We've both seen how that kind of life isn't compatible with long-term relationships.'

'You're. Just. Having. Sex,' Diana reiterated.

'Oh, come on, Diana, you know I'm not good at that. The last guy I was just having sex with I ended up engaged to.'

Diana nodded. 'And the sex was lousy.'

'Hey,' Stella protested. 'It wasn't lousy, it was…nice. Sweet. It may not have been…imaginative but it could have been worse.' Her friend didn't look convinced. 'He was a pretty straight guy, Diana. Not all men want to have sex hanging from the chandeliers. There's nothing wrong with sweet.'

'No, absolutely not,' she agreed. 'Except you did write a book full of hot, sweaty, dirty, pirate sex during your time with Dale.' She shrugged. 'I'm no psychologist but I think they call that transference.'

'*They*,' Stella said, bugging her eyes at her friend, 'call it *fiction*.'

Diana held up her hands in surrender. 'All right, all right. I'm just saying…you're going to be on that boat with him for long periods of time where there'll be nothing to do…it might be worth thinking about, is all…'

Stella shook her head at her incorrigible friend. 'I'll be writing.'

Diana laughed. 'Good answer.'

At two Stella hugged Diana ferociously and thanked her for locking up after them. She was staying on for another night to get some work done far from the distractions of London.

'I promise I'll come back with a book,' she whispered to her friend. 'The ideas are already popping. Tell Joy she's going to love Lucinda.'

Diana laughed. 'Joy will be overjoyed.'

Stella grimaced. She hoped so. She'd added a decade to her very patient editor's life and she *owed* Joy this. Not just a book, but a book to rival Vasco's. She scurried to Rick's hire car with her bag, hoping they made it out of Cornwall before another storm blew in.

Rick pulled up beside Diana and smiled at her. 'See ya later, Miss Kitty. It was nice spending some time with you,' he said.

Diana nodded distractedly, bobbing her head back and forth to see what Stella was up to.

Rick frowned. These two women were hard on his ego. 'I know Stel values your friendship and—'

'Yeh, yeh,' Diana said, cutting him off and dragging him back inside the cottage. She pulled her dog-eared copy of *Pleasure Hunt* from her handbag on the hall stand and thrust it at him. 'Take it. Read it. You won't be disappointed.'

Rick frowned down at the cover he recognised from earlier. 'Er, it's really not my thing.'

'Trust me. It's your thing.' She glanced over Rick's shoulder, knowing that Stella would kill her if she even had an inkling of what Diana was doing. 'It's really quite…illuminating.'

'Okay.'

He ran his fingers over the raised gold lettering that spelt out Stella's name. He felt a surge of pride that Stel had made a path for herself in the world—something that rocked her boat. He knew that Nathan had been immensely proud of his little girl's success.

'Thanks,' he said as he tucked it under his arm and backed out of the cottage.

'Stop,' Diana hissed. 'What are you doing?' She whisked

it out from under his arm, spun him around, unzipped his backpack and shoved it deep inside.

'She's sensitive about it,' Diana explained as Rick gave her a questioning look. 'Do not read it around her. And if she springs you—I will deny all knowledge of how you came by it. Capiche?'

Rick chuckled as he held up his hands in surrender. 'Sure. Okay.'

He took a couple of tentative paces out of the cottage, expecting to be yanked back inside again. It wasn't until he was halfway to the car that he started to relax.

He smiled to himself. *God, but he loved women.*

Five hours later they were airborne and Rick was busily flirting with the air hostess. Stella wasn't sure why she was so annoyed. After all, she'd seen Rick in action with women nearly all of her life.

Maybe it was just the relentless afternoon of it. The woman at the petrol station. The one at the rental desk. Another at the check-in lounge. Oh, and the coffee shop—and she'd have to have been in her sixties. It seemed there wasn't a woman in existence who wasn't fair game for his laid-back style of flirting.

Including her.

But she was used to his casual, flirty banter. She knew it was harmless and she could give as good as she got.

The women of the world were not.

'Champagne?' Rick asked her.

It was tempting but after last night her liver probably needed a break. 'No, thanks,' she said, smiling at the hostess, who she was pretty sure actually didn't give a damn if Stella wanted a drink or not.

Rick watched the swagger of the stewardess's hips in her tight pencil skirt as she left to grab his beer. Stella rolled her eyes at him and he grinned. 'So,' he said, snuggling down further into the comfortable leather seat. 'You haven't asked how the business is going.'

Stella pulled the blind down on her window. 'Well, we're in business class so I'm assuming it's all going okay.'

Rick nodded. 'It is.'

Stella sighed. 'Rick, I told you at the wake that whatever decisions you wanted to make were fine by me. That I only wanted to be a silent partner. You've been half of the business since you were fifteen. It's been *your* blood, sweat and tears that helped to build it to where it is today. Dad should have left his half to you, not me. It should be all yours.'

Rick looked askance, his blue eyes flashing. 'Stel, what is a man worth if he cannot provide for his family?' he said, his voice laced with reproach and sounding remarkably Spanish all of a sudden. 'The business was Nathan's legacy and he knew how much you loved it. Of course he wanted it to go to you. Of course he wanted to leave you with no financial worries.'

She raised an eyebrow. 'Do you have any idea how much money my book has made?'

Rick thought about the contraband copy of *Pleasure Hunt* secreted away in his backpack. 'No. But the business has a multimillion-dollar turnover annually and whether you need it or not—half of it's yours.'

'I know…I'm just saying, I can look after myself.'

He nodded. 'I know that. I've always known that.'

Stella's breath caught in her throat at the sincerity in his tropical eyes. His shoulder-length hair fell forward to form a partial curtain around his face and, with his slight sideways position, she felt as if they were cut off from the rest of the aeroplane.

'Your beer, sir.'

Stella glanced up at the stewardess and was surprised to feel Rick's gaze linger on her face. She looked back at him quizzically and they just looked at each other for a long mo-

ment before he smiled at her, then turned to accept the offering.

He started to chat with the stewardess again and Stella
turned away. She shut her eyes, not wanting to hear the banter that fell so easily from those wicked Vasco lips.

It was a long flight. She might as well try and get some
sleep.

She woke a few hours later feeling miraculously refreshed.
Rick was stretched out asleep in his chair, his face turned towards her, those killer sable lashes throwing shadows on his
cheeks.

For a moment she just stared at him, at his utter beauty.
He'd always been good-looking but age had turned all that
brash youthful charisma into a deep and abiding sex appeal.

The urge to push his hair back off his forehead where it
had fallen in haphazard array almost trumped the urge to
trace his lips with her finger. They looked all soft and slack
in slumber but she knew, without ever having experienced it,
that they would be just the right amount of hard at precisely
the right time—like Vasco's.

She'd come perilously close to knowing it for real. Could
still remember the way her pulse had roared, her eyes had
fluttered closed as he'd leaned in to make good on her dare
and fulfil all her teenage fantasies.

And, courtesy of a crush bigger than the United Kingdom,
there'd been plenty of them.

Fantasies that had seen her tick each day down on a calen-
dar as the holidays had approached, her foolish heart tripping
every time she'd thought about those blue, blue eyes and all
that bare, broad, bronzed skin courtesy of his Spanish mother.

All the time hoping that it would be this summer he'd see
her as a woman instead of a girl. That he'd make good on the
increasingly confusing signals he sent and act instead of tease.

And the eve of her sixteenth birthday all that breathless longing had come to fruition.

'Sweet sixteen and never been kissed,' he'd teased.

He'd been nearly nineteen and so much more experienced. She'd watched him flirt with girls since he'd been thirteen and been aware of his effect on them for much longer than he had.

She'd screwed up her courage. 'Maybe you should do something about that?' she'd murmured, her heart hammering.

She'd watched as his Adam's apple had bobbed and his gaze had briefly fallen to her mouth. 'Yeh, right,' he'd dismissed.

She'd smiled at him and said the one thing she'd known would work. 'I dare you.'

And it had worked. She'd seen something inside him give as his gaze had zeroed in on her mouth and his lips had moved closer.

Her father's curt 'Riccardo!' had been the bucket of water they'd both needed.

A reminder that there was a line between them that should never be crossed no matter how close they'd danced to it.

And she was glad for it now.

Glad that this magnificent man liked her and enjoyed her company and called her his friend. That he could drop by out of the blue and use her shower and doss down for the night and there was no awkward history, no uncomfortable silences.

Despite what Diana thought, a person didn't die of sexual frustration and she wouldn't sacrifice their friendship and mutual respect for a brief slaking of bodily desires.

No matter how damn good she knew it would be.

He stirred and she froze, hoping like crazy that lazy blue gaze wasn't about to blast her in tropical heat.

It didn't. But it was enough to spur her into action. She was not going to sit here and ogle him as if she were still in the midst of her teenage crush, watching him surreptitiously from behind her dark sunglasses as he went about the business of running a boat.

Without a shirt.
Always without a shirt.
She pulled out her laptop and powered it up.

An hour later the cabin crew came through offering a meal and Rick woke. He stretched, then righted his chair, glancing over at Stella busily tapping away. She seemed engrossed and he smiled at her.

'I thought you were blocked.'

Stella looked up from her notes. 'I've had an idea,' she admitted.

'Hah!' he crowed. 'I told you all you needed was a treasure hunt.'

'Yeh, well, all I'm doing is some preliminary planning, at the moment. It remains to be seen if I can actually write anything.'

Although she knew she could. In fact she itched to. Lucinda and Inigo's story was becoming clearer and clearer.

'So how does that work, then? Writer's block?' he asked.

She shrugged. 'I look at a blank page all day terrified that I'm not good enough, that I'm a one-book wonder, willing the words to come and when, on a good day, some actually do appear, they're all crap and I delete them.'

Rick nodded thoughtfully. He couldn't say that he understood exactly, but he could see the consternation creasing her brow and the look he'd seen in her eyes last night akin to panic. The same look he'd sometimes seen when she'd been a kid and Nathan had been late returning to the surface.

'Maybe you need to give yourself permission to be crap?' he suggested. 'Just get it all down, warts and all. Switch your internal editor off?'

Stella raised an eyebrow at him. 'Did Diana tell you to say that?'

Rick chuckled. 'No.'

'Well, it's easier said than done, believe me.' She sighed.

'I think if I'd had a whole bunch of books rejected before *Pleasure Hunt*, then I'd have known stuff like that. But this crazy instant success didn't give me any time to fail or any time to know who I am as a writer. I think I needed this time to figure that out.'

Rick nodded. 'So...' he said, looking over her shoulder, 'are you going to tell me what it's about?'

Stella shut the lid of her laptop. 'Nope.'

The last time a guy had realised what she'd written it hadn't ended well.

'Excuse me, Ms Mills?'

Stella looked up at a stewardess who had brought her some water earlier. 'Yes?'

'I'm sorry, I hope you don't mind—I saw your name on the passenger list and I just finished reading *Pleasure Hunt*.' She held it up. 'Would you mind signing it for me?'

Stella blushed. 'Certainly,' she murmured as she held her hand out for the book and proffered pen. 'Is there any message in particular you'd like me to write?'

'Just to me, Andrea.' The stewardess smiled.

Stella wrote a brief message to Andrea, then signed her name with a flourish before handing the book and pen back.

'Thank you so much,' Andrea said. 'I shall cherish it.'

'Thank *you*,' Stella replied. 'It's always nice to meet people who like what you do.'

Andrea nodded. 'I better go and serve dinner or my little band of travellers won't be happy.'

Stella and Rick watched her walk away. He turned to her. 'Wow. You're seriously famous, aren't you?'

Stella chuckled. 'Does that threaten your masculinity?' It had certainly threatened Dale's.

'Hell, no.' He grinned. 'I'm a little turned on, actually.'

Stella shook her head. 'If you're thinking threesome, forget it.'

Rick laughed. 'Well, I am now.'

CHAPTER THREE

STELLA had been seven and Rick ten when they'd first laid eyes on the *Dolphin* anchored at St Kitts. They'd both stood on the bow of the *Persephone* with their mouths open, staring at the wooden beauty. Teak, oak, cypress and the original brass fittings had given her an old-world charm hinting at an era when craftsmanship was everything and things were made to last.

Stella still remembered Rick's awed whisper. 'One day she's going to be mine.'

And as they stood on the wharf looking down at her now, the brass gleaming beneath a high Aussie sun, the wooden deck warm and inviting, she looked as grand and majestic as ever.

Lucinda sighed in her head.

'God, Rick,' Stella breathed, that same stirring in her blood she always felt with a stiff sea breeze ruffling her hair. 'She's even more beautiful than I remembered.'

Rick looked down at her, her hair streaming behind her, her pink lips parted in awe. She'd changed into a vest top and cut-off denim shorts and she was so tiny the urge to tuck her under his arm took him by surprise.

'Yes, she is,' he murmured, looking back at his purchase.

Stella looked up at him. The sea breeze whipped his long pirate locks across his face. His strong jaw was dark with stubble. 'She must have cost you a fortune.'

He shrugged. 'Some things are beyond money. And she's worth every cent.'

She nodded, looking back at the superbly crafted boat. 'Why now?' she asked.

He shrugged. 'I listened to your father talk about *The Mermaid* all my life. About how one day he was going to find Inigo's final resting place. And then he died without ever having seen it.'

Rick felt a swell of emotion in his chest and stopped. He slid an arm around her shoulders and pulled her gently into his side. 'I always thought Nathan was invincible...'

Stella snaked an arm around his waist, her heart twisting as his words ran out. She'd always thought so too. Always thought her father would be like Captain Ahab, *The Mermaid* his white whale. They both stood on the dock watching the gentle bob of the *Dolphin* for a few moments.

'I've dreamt about owning this boat since I was ten years old,' Rick murmured, finding his voice again. 'I didn't want to wait any longer.'

Stella nodded, feeling a deep and abiding affinity with Rick that couldn't have been stronger had they been bound by blood.

That wouldn't have been possible had they been lovers.

'Besides,' he grinned, giving her a quick squeeze before letting her go, 'the *company* owns it.'

Stella laughed. 'Oh, really, creative accounting, huh?'

'Something like that,' he laughed.

'So she's actually half mine?' she teased.

Rick threw his backpack on deck and jumped on board. He held out his hand. *'Mi casa es su casa,'* he murmured.

Stella's breath hitched as she took his hand. He spoke Spanish impeccably and with that bronzed colouring and those impossibly blue eyes he was every inch the Spaniard. He might have an English father and have gone to English schools but for his formative years he was raised by his Romany grandmother and she'd made sure her Riccardo had been immersed in the lingo.

As she stepped aboard she checked out the small motorised dinghy hanging from a frame attached to the stern above the water line. Then her gaze fell to the starboard hull where the bold gold lettering outlined in fine black detail proclaimed a change of name. She almost tripped and stumbled into him.

'Whoa there,' he said, holding her hips to steady her. They curved out from her waist and he had to remind himself that the flesh beneath his palms was Stella's. 'You've turned into a real landlubber, haven't you?' he teased.

She stared at him for a moment. 'You changed her name?' she asked breathlessly.

He shrugged as he smiled down at her flummoxed face. 'I promised you.'

Stella thumped his arm and ignored his theatrical recoil. 'I was seven years old,' she yelled.

She stormed to the edge and looked over at the six yellow letters, her eyes filling with tears.

Stella.

'You don't like it?'

She blinked her tears away and marched back to him and thumped his chest this time. 'I love it, you idiot! It's the nicest thing anyone's ever done for me.' Then she threw herself into his arms.

Not even her father had named a boat after her.

Rick chuckled as he lifted her feet off the ground and hugged her back, his senses infusing with coconut.

'I can't believe you did that,' she said, her voice muffled against a pec. She pushed against the bands of his arms and squirmed away from him.

'I told you I would.'

Stella had forgotten, but she remembered it now as if it were yesterday. Rick talking incessantly about buying the *Dolphin* that summer they'd first seen her and her making him promise that if he did he'd rename it after her.

'I didn't think you *actually* would,' she said incredulously.

'Anything for my favourite girl,' he quipped.

She ignored his easy line as she'd ignored all his others. 'You should have said no. I was a brat.'

He nodded. 'Yes, you were.'

She gave him another playful thump but smiled up at him just the same. He smiled back and for a moment they just stood there, the joy of a shared memory uniting them.

'Well, come on, then,' she said after a moment. 'Show me around.'

A spiral stairway led to a below deck that was far better than Stella had imagined in her wildest dreams. Polished wood invited her to run her hands along its surfaces. Brass fittings gleamed from every nook and cranny. The spacious area was dominated by ceiling beams, heavy brocade curtains over the portholes, oriental rugs and dark leather chairs.

It wasn't lavish—she'd seen plenty of lavish interiors in her time—but it *was* very masculine, the addition of Rick even more so. He looked completely at home in this nautical nirvana and for a moment Stella could imagine him in a half-undone silk shirt and breeches, sprawled out down here, knocking back some rum after a hard day's seafaring.

She blinked as Rick segued into Vasco.

'Saloon here, galley over there,' he said, thumbing over his shoulder where she could see a glimpse of stainless steel. 'Engine room…' he stamped his foot '…below us. Forward and aft cabins both have en suites. I thought you might like the aft cabin? It's slightly bigger.'

'Sure.' She shrugged, her pulse tripping madly at her bizarre vision. 'That sounds fine.'

Rick, who'd only seen photographs of the finished product himself, sat in a chair. He ran his hand over the decadent leather. 'Wow, they've done a magnificent job.'

Stella blinked again as she looked down on him for once. If ever there was magnificent it was him, sitting in that chair, captain of all he surveyed. It reminded her of the scene in *Pleasure Hunt* where Lady Mary finally capitulated to his touch. Where she realised, after a particularly harrowing raid, life was short and she didn't want to die without having known the touch of a truly sensual man.

She stood in front of Vasco in the privacy of his cabin as he sat, thighs insolently spread, in his chair, caressing the arm as if it were the breast of a beautiful woman. She looked down at him, waiting. When he leant forward and reached under her skirts she didn't protest, nor when he placed his hands on the backs of her thighs and pulled her onto his lap so she was straddling him, her skirts frothing around her.

'It's so much better than the photos,' Rick murmured.

Stella blinked as his voice dragged her back to the present. She took a step back as the vivid image of Vasco played large in her mind.

'It's amazing, Rick,' she agreed. 'Just…incredible.'

Rick smiled at her as his hand continued to stroke the leather. He was pleased Stella was here to share this moment with him. This boat, more than any of the ones they'd been on over the years, connected them in a way only shared childhood dreams could.

'Let's take her out,' he said, standing. The sudden urge to hoist a sail and go where the wind took him shot through his veins like the first sip of beer on a hot summer day.

'I know we should be provisioning her for our trip but we can do that tomorrow. Let's take her over to Green Island. Give her a good run. We can go snorkelling. We have the basics here…well, we have beer anyway…and we can catch some fish and anchor there for the night. I want to lie on the deck and look at the stars like we used to do when we were kids.'

'Sure,' she agreed readily. Anything, anything to get her out of this saloon and far away from the fantasy.

Where the hell was her filter? She did not fantasise about Rick.

Not in front of him anyway.

'Fabulous idea. Can I take her once she's out of the harbour?'

Stella had learned to sail practically before she could walk. Her father had seen to that. Hell, so had her mother, a keen sailor in her own right, but it had been a lot of years since she'd been on the open sea.

'You still remember what to do?' Rick teased.

She smiled at him. 'I'm sure it'll come back to me. It's just like riding a bike, yes?'

Or having sex.

Diana had assured her you didn't forget how to do that either.

'Don't worry, I'll be there to guide you. Do you trust me?'

Yep…exactly what Vasco had said to Lady Mary.

Do you trust me?

Stella swallowed. 'I trust that you don't want me to run your very expensive boat—sorry, the *company's* very expensive boat—onto a reef,' she quipped.

Rick laughed. 'You have that right. Come on, first mate, let's get this show on the road.'

Within half an hour they were under way, out on the open ocean, and Stella couldn't remember the last time she'd felt this alive. She'd waited patiently while Rick had used the motor to manoeuvre out of the harbour, then helped him with the still familiar motions of putting up the sails. She heard Lucinda sigh as they billowed with the moderate breeze and her pulse leapt as the boat surged forward, slicing across the whitecaps.

Rick, who had taken his shirt off—of course—stood behind her at the wheel for the first ten minutes, giving her a quick refresher. It wasn't needed. Her feel for the boat was instantaneous, like the familiarity of her own heartbeat, and even if it hadn't been they could easily have switched to the sophisticated autopilot system guided by the satellite technology that he'd had installed as part of the fully computerised upgrade.

But it was exhilarating to feel the pulse of the ocean beneath her feet again. She shut her eyes, raised her face to the sun as the big wheel in her hands felt like a natural extension of her being. In her mind's eye she could see Lucinda laughing up at her as she undulated through the waves, riding the bow with the dolphins.

Rick looked up from tying down a loose rope and caught her in her sun-worshipping stance. He'd worried that buying the *Dolphin* on a whim had been a mistake, an indulgence he didn't have the time to realise, a reaction to Nathan's sudden death.

But he didn't any more.

Nathan's *accident* had rocked him to his very core. He'd been there that day. Had seen Nathan's lifeless form, minus his breathing apparatus, bob to the surface. Had frantically dragged him aboard, puffed air into lungs that had been consumed by sea water too many minutes before.

Had demanded that he stay with him.

Stay *for* him.

Stay for Stella.

His own father's memory had faded to nothing over the years. He'd been too young when his father's regular bouts of drunken shore leave had caught up with him. Just a few faded photographs and the oft-repeated stories that got more and more fantastical late into the night after one too many beers.

Anthony Granville had occupied a legendary status amongst the men that knew him but he'd still got himself dead.

It was Nathan who'd been Rick's role model. His stand-in father. And Nathan who had taken on his full-time guardianship when he was a tearaway fifteen-year-old and his grandmother had washed her hands of him.

Rick had only ever wanted to be at sea managing his half of the business. And Nathan had facilitated it.

But he hadn't made it easy—oh, no.

Nathan had been a tough task master.

Rick had thought his days of schooling and routine were done but Nathan had been worse than his grandmother. Nathan had insisted that he do his schooling by correspondence. And when he was done with that for the day, he'd given him every lousy job possible.

Had worked him like a navvy.

And Rick couldn't be more grateful. In his own way, Nathan had given him a better grounding than if he'd grown up in a loving, two-parent secure home.

He'd been so angry with Nathan when he'd landed in the UK thirty hours after they'd given up trying to resuscitate him.

Angry that Nathan had left him to be the bearer of bad news.

Angry that he'd left full stop.

But he'd known the news had to come from him.

The thought of someone else telling Linda—telling Stella—had been completely unpalatable. Nathan would have wanted it to be him and he hadn't wanted it to come from anyone else.

How could he have let some faceless policeman tell Linda? She and Nathan might have been divorced but even Rick had been able to see the deep and abiding love she still felt for him.

And there was no way he'd have let anyone else tell Stella.

The autopsy results just prior to the funeral had made Nathan's death more palatable. Rick had understood, as a man of the sea himself, that Nathan had chosen the ocean over a hospital.

But it hadn't lessened his loss.

And his very impulsive purchase of the *Dolphin* was so

mixed up in the whole vortex of grief he just hadn't been sure of his motivations.

But, as she opened her eyes and smiled at him as if she were riding a magic carpet instead of some very tame waves, he was one hundred per cent sure.

The *Dolphin* was part of them. Their history. And whatever else happened over the years in their lives, it would always bond them together, always be theirs—his, hers and Nathan's.

It had been quite a few years since Stella had been snorkelling. But as they lay anchor a couple of hours later crystalline tropical waters the exact shade of Rick's eyes beckoned, and she was below deck and back up again in record speed.

'What on earth are you wearing?' Rick demanded as she appeared by his side while he was rummaging around in a storage compartment for some goggles and fins.

Stella looked down at her very sensible one-piece. 'You don't like the colour?' she asked.

He tisked to cover the fact that he didn't give a damn what colour it was. 'It's stinger season, Stel. There should be a wetsuit hanging on the back of your cabin door and a stinger suit in one of the drawers.'

Stella looked at the water, desperate to feel it on her skin with no barriers just as she had in her Lucinda dream.

'Oh, come on,' she protested. 'We'd be pretty protected out here on the reef, surely?'

'I'll be sure to tell them that's what you thought when they're giving you the anti-venin.'

Stella shrugged. 'I'm willing to risk it.'

Rick shook his head emphatically. 'I'm not.'

He worked in an inherently dangerous field—there were a lot of things in the ocean that could kill a man—and his reputation for safety was second to none. He certainly wasn't going to have to explain to Linda that he'd let her daughter die too.

He pointed to the stairs leading to the lower deck. 'Go,' he intoned.

Stella rolled her eyes. 'Yeh, yeh.'

'Don't make me come down there,' he threatened.

Stella felt the flirty threat right down to her toes. What would he say if she challenged him to do just that?

Rick smiled to himself as she slunk away, her one-piece riding up the cheek of one buttock. He looked away. When she reappeared a few minutes later she was zipped into light blue neck-to-ankle Lycra.

'I hate these things,' she complained as she pulled at the clinging fabric. 'I look like a dumpling.'

Rick deliberately didn't look. What Nathan's daughter did or did not look like poured into a stinger suit was none of his business. He was still trying to not think about that half-exposed butt cheek.

'Everyone does,' he said, handing her some flippers and her mask and snorkel.

Stella glared at him. No, not everyone did. Not size-zero six-foot supermodels. Which she wasn't. And certainly not him, half zipped into his, his thighs outlined to perfection, the narrowness of his hips a stark contrast to the roundness of her own. *He* looked like an Yves St Laurent cologne guy or James freaking Bond walking out of the Mediterranean in his teeny tiny swimming trunks.

She fitted her mask to her head and looked at him. 'Aren't you coming?' she asked, staring pointedly at his state of undress.

'Right behind you,' he said.

They snorkelled on and off for most of the afternoon. They stopped a couple of times to grab a drink of water and Rick found his state-of-the-art underwater camera but otherwise they frolicked in the warm tropical waters for hours as if they were kids again playing pirates and mermaids.

She'd forgotten just how magical it was with the sun beating on her back and her head immersed in an enchanted underworld kingdom. Where fish all the colours of the rainbow darted around her and cavorted amongst coral that formed a unique and fascinating underwater garden.

Where the dark shadows of huge manta rays and small reef sharks hovered in the distance.

Where the silence made the beauty that much more profound.

It was after five o'clock when they called it a day. Stella threw on her clothes from earlier; Rick just unzipped his suit to his waist and looked all James Bond again. They threw some fishing lines in to catch their dinner while they drank cold beer and looked at Rick's pictures on her laptop. They laughed and reminisced and Rick showed her the pictures from their latest salvage—a nineteenth-century frigate off the Virgin Islands.

They caught two decent-sized coral trout and he cooked them on a small portable grill plate he'd brought up from below. It melted in their mouths as they dangled their legs over the side and watched the blush of twilight slowly creep across the sky to the gentle slap of waves against the hull.

Stella could feel the fatigue of jet lag catching up with her as the balmy breeze blew her drying hair into a no-doubt completely unattractive bird's nest.

That was the one good thing about hanging out with a guy who'd known you for ever—he'd seen her looking worse.

Rick took her plate away and she collapsed back against the deck, knees bent, looking up at the stars as they slowly, one by one, appeared before her eyes. She could hear the clank of dishes below and by the time Rick rejoined her night had completely claimed the heavens and a mass of diamond pricks winked above them.

A three-quarter moon hung low in the sky, casting a trail of moonbeams on the ocean surface.

'Are you awake, sleepy head?' Rick asked as he approached.

She countered his question with one of her own. 'Is it waxing or waning?' she asked, knowing that a man of the sea knew those things without ever having to look at a tide chart—it was in their DNA.

'Waxing,' Rick confirmed as he took up position beside her, lying back against the sun-warmed wood, also staring towards the heavens. He'd taken his stinger suit off and was wearing just his boardies.

Stella sighed. 'It's so beautiful. I bet you never get sick of this.'

'Nope. Never.'

He'd spent countless hours on deck at night, with Nathan teaching him how to navigate by the stars. He supposed to some, even back then, it had seemed hopelessly old-fashioned with all the sophisticated GPS systems and autopilot technology that had been around in the salvage industry for decades, but it had got him out of trouble more than once when satellites had been down or equipment had failed.

And he'd loved listening to the awe in Nathan's voice as he'd talked about the heavens as if each star were a friend. He hadn't just known their shape or the positions in relation to the horizon, but he'd known all the old seafaring legends about them and told them in such a way that had held Rick enthralled.

Nathan's celestial knowledge had been encyclopaedic and Rick had soaked it up like a sponge.

And then he'd regurgitated it to an awestruck Stella, who'd hung on his every word.

How many hours had they spent as kids lying on their backs on the deck of a boat pointing out different constellations, waiting with bated breath for the first shooting star of the night?

Her arm brushed his as she pointed at the Southern Cross and he realised he'd missed this.

This…companionship.

The last time they'd done it was the summer she'd finished school for good. A year after that near kiss. She'd alternated between giddiness at the freedom of it all and distraction over her impending results. They'd lain together on deck and looked up into the diamond studded abyss and he'd told her if they saw a shooting star it would be a sign that she'd passed.

No sooner had he spoken the words than a white streak trailed its incandescent light across the heavens right above them. She'd gasped and he'd told her to shut her eyes and wish upon it and watched her as she did.

Yep. He'd missed this.

God knew he'd had a lot of women in exactly this position over the years but this was different. For a start he hadn't been remotely interested in looking at the stars with any of them. Although to be fair, as his relationship with Stella had teetered on the brink of something neither of them had been game enough to define during their teen years, he hadn't exactly had his head in the stars with her either.

But he did tonight. Stella somehow seemed to bring out the amateur astronomer in him.

And it was…nice.

No agenda. No pressure. No expectations.

Just two old friends relaxing after the perfect day.

'Hey,' Stella said, extending her neck right back as her peripheral vision caught a moonbeam illuminating a chunk of metal hanging off some kind of a fixed pole at the stern. She squinted. 'Is that a shower head?'

Rick extended his neck too and smiled. 'Yep. I've always wanted to be able to take a shower under the stars.' He grinned, relaxing his neck back to a more neutral position.

She laughed as she also released the abnormal stretch, returning to her inspection of the night sky. 'Well, you've thought of everything, haven't you?'

He nodded. 'I've been thinking about this boat for a lot of years.'

They fell silent for a moment, letting the slap of waves against the hull serenade them as their gazes roamed the magnificence of the celestial display.

Stella's yawn broke the natural rhythm. 'I'm beat.' She shut her eyes. 'All that sun and sea on top of the jet lag is a deadly combination.'

'You can't go to bed before we see a shooting star, Stel. Look.' He nudged her shoulder. 'There's Gemini.'

Stella's eyes flicked open and she dutifully followed the path of a perfectly formed bicep all the way to the tip of his raised index finger. She tutted. 'You always had a thing for Gemini.'

He grinned. 'What's not to like about two chicks?'

They laughed and just as he was lowering his arm it happened: a trail of light shot across the night sky, burning bright for long seconds.

Stella gasped and Rick whispered, 'Quick, make a wish.'

Stella thought about Lucinda and Inigo. And dear Joy with the patience of Job. She squeezed her eyes shut as the light faded into extinction and wished for another blockbuster.

Rick turned his head and watched her eye-scrunching concentration. 'What'd you wish for?' he asked.

Stella opened her eyes, her breath catching in her throat at their closeness. Even with the dark pressing in around them, his blue eyes seemed to pierce right into her soul. 'It's a secret,' she murmured. 'If I tell you it won't come true.'

He shook his head. 'You always were a romantic. I should have known you'd go on to write romance novels.'

His voice was light and teasing and not full of scorn as Dale's had been. Dale had been barely able to say the R word. She smiled. 'Says he who insisted I wait to wish upon a star,' she countered.

He laughed. 'Touché.'

His laugh did funny things to her insides and a part of her wanted to stay out with him all night and watch the sun come up, but her eyelids were growing heavier and she yawned again.

She sat. 'Right. I'm off to bed.' She stood and looked down at him lying on the deck of his boat wearing nothing but a pair of low-slung boardies and still somehow managing to look as if he ruled the entire ocean. 'See you in the morning.'

He nodded. 'I won't be too far behind you,' he murmured.

Stella turned away from him, padding her way across the deck, conscious of his eyes on her. She heard his faint 'Night, Stel' reach her as she climbed down the stairs.

She was too beat to reply as her legs took her past the galley, through the saloon to the aft cabin where Rick must have placed her luggage earlier. She didn't bother to shower, hell, she barely bothered to undress, just kicked out of her shorts, pulled the sheets back and crawled under.

She was dreaming even before her head hit the pillow.

Dreaming of Vasco.

CHAPTER FOUR

It was ten the next morning before Stella woke. The gentle rhythm of the waves had rocked her into a deep, jet-lagged slumber. She had a quick shower and threw on a sarong and T-shirt. Rick wasn't below deck but there was an incredible aroma coming from above and she followed her nose.

He was standing at the grill in his boardies—no shirt—and for a moment she just watched the broad bronzed planes of his back that narrowed the closer they got to his waistband.

Or perhaps hip-band might have been more salient.

But then her stomach outed her by growling loudly and she propelled herself forward. 'Sorry for sleeping so late,' she said as she approached him.

Rick turned and smiled at her. 'It's fine—jet lag's a bitch like that. I've only been up for half an hour myself. But, lucky for us—' his smiled broadened into a grin '—the fish have been up for a while.'

Stella inhaled. 'Hmm. Smells great.'

'Grab some plates—we'll eat, then get back to the marina.'

They ate quickly and were under way half an hour later, Rick again letting Stella take the wheel. It was early afternoon before they were finally on land again and alighting a taxi at Cairns Central Shopping Centre.

'So you think you can remember how to provision a boat for a few weeks?'

Stella nodded. She'd often gone with Sergio to buy supplies just prior to an expedition. Serg, a grizzled veteran of the merchant navy and stalwart of Mills and Granville, usually went out on the longer trips as chief cook and bottle washer. He cooked good plain food in bulk and pastry to die for.

'I checked out the galley properly so I know what storage capabilities there are. I assume we'll buy fresh food where we can along the way?'

'Yep.'

'So I'll get all the usual staples.'

He handed over the company credit card of which she was a signatory. 'Where are you going?' she asked as she slid the plastic into the back pocket of her shorts.

'I'm heading to the Boating, Camping, Fishing store to pick up a few things. Let's meet up back here at that coffee shop,' he said, pointing behind her, 'in about an hour?'

Stella checked her watch. 'Right. See you then.'

Shopping in another country was always a challenge. In Penzance she frequented the local supermarket and she knew what and where everything was. Far from home, it took her much longer to find the things she'd already put on a mental list in her head.

But at least Cairns had first-world shopping facilities and everyone spoke the same language. She and Serg had certainly shopped in much more rudimentary surrounds.

By the time the hour was up Stella had a trolley piled high with provisions and the credit card had taken a hit—if they were going to be limited in what they ate for the next few weeks, then she was going to make damn sure what they did have was of the highest quality. Good chocolate—for her anyway, Rick wasn't fussy—and the most decadent biscuits money could buy—for him.

Serg had told her when she was a teenager that Rick had a sweet tooth that was best kept fed. She hadn't been sure whether that had some double meaning or not, but it had certainly fed *her* hormone-fuelled imagination.

Stella pushed the uncooperative metal beast with two wonky wheels for what seemed like five miles in the giant sprawling shopping centre. She almost crashed into a shop window and earned the wrath of a mother who thought Stella was deliberately trying to run her tantrumming little angel down.

When she finally reached the coffee shop her abdominals, quads and biceps were cramped with the effort of keeping the damn thing on track. Her mood was not great. It didn't improve any to find Rick, with one shopping bag, chatting up a tall, dark-haired waitress who looked as if she were born dancing the Flamenco.

Of course.

The man had a perpetual hard-on.

'Hi,' she said, using the back of Rick's chair as a brake for the trolley.

Rick spun around as the impact interrupted him mid-flirt.

'Oops, sorry, damn thing is impossible to control,' she said, smiling sweetly at the waitress, who looked as if she was about to give Stella a piece of her mind for careening into a customer.

A sex-god customer.

Stella was pretty damn sure if someone had barged into her chair with a dangerous weapon, Ms Flamenco wouldn't have batted an eyelid.

'Hey, Stel.' He grinned. 'Have a seat. You want a coffee? Something to eat? Ramona says they do a mean nachos here.'

Stella smiled at Ramona. 'Nachos and a flat white would be great, thanks.'

Ramona nodded at Rick. 'I'll be back in a jiffy.'

I just bet you will, Stella thought uncharitably as she sat down.

'Whoa, you buy the whole shop?' Rick asked, examining the contents of the missile that had smacked into him.

'You have to cover every contingency,' she said waspishly.

'Ooh, Snickers,' he said, pulling out the packet of fun-sized chocolate bars. 'My favourite.'

Yes. Which was why she'd bought them.

'Can I take your order, sir?'

Stella looked up at another goddess smiling down at Rick as if he'd invented oxygen. Lord, where did this coffee shop source their staff from—www.lookgoodnaked.com?

'We've ordered,' she said tersely.

'Sorry.' Rick smiled and shrugged.

'No worries,' the woman said, her smile not wavering, her gaze not leaving his. 'If you need anything just yell. I'm Holly.'

'Thanks, I'll holler, Holly,' he said and she giggled.

Stella rolled her eyes. 'You're incorrigible.'

Rick grinned. 'I have no idea what you're talking about.'

Stella ignored him, instead choosing to go through the docket with him for anything she might have forgotten while they waited for their meal. It was going to be too late once they'd cast off in the morning. No less than two waitresses interrupted them while they did so.

Their meals finally arrived and Stella almost laughed as yet another woman, a leggy redhead, delivered them.

Were they drawing straws?

This one looked older—older than Rick for sure—and had the calm authority and predatory grace of a woman who knew what she liked. She introduced herself as the owner.

'Ramona was saying you're sailing north for a few weeks. I don't suppose you need a deckhand?' she joked as she placed Rick's meal in front of him.

'I'm the deckhand,' Stella intoned.

Was she invisible?

Was it that ridiculous to think that she could be his girl-friend? It seemed every female employee in the coffee shop thought so, if their quick dismissive gazes followed by their unabashed flirting were any indication.

She wanted to stand up and say, *Hey, I'm a famous author,*

don't you know. But then Rick looked at her and winked and she felt as if he'd just ruffled her hair and slipped her a few bucks to run along and leave him do his thing.

She felt like his kid sister.

'Do you know boats?' Rick asked.

The woman smiled. 'Oh, yes, my ex always owned classic yachts. I hear yours is a beauty.'

Rick nodded enthusiastically. 'You should drop by the marina and see her. The *Stella* is a true class act.'

Stella blinked.

Had he just invited a cougar back to the boat?

Oh, no, don't mind me.

The woman smiled at him. 'I may just do that.'

'Can I get some cracked pepper?' Stella asked.

The redhead gave her a cursory once-over and disregarded her in less than five seconds. 'I'll send Ramona over,' she said and she slunk away.

'God, this looks good, doesn't it?' Rick asked as he turned his attention to his meal.

Stella had suddenly lost her appetite. Sometimes she just couldn't work him out. The man knew he was attractive to women. She'd seen him work that to his advantage too many times to class him as clueless, but she didn't think he truly understood how effortlessly it worked in his favour.

Even when he wasn't trying, women flocked. And of that, he was totally unaware. She was sure of it.

She picked at her meal and was pleased when they managed to leave the coffee shop unmolested forty-five minutes later. He took the trolley, managing it like the flocks of women—effortlessly—and they caught a taxi back to the marina.

Once on board they stocked the galley with the supplies then sat at the dining table drinking beer and plotting their course. Stella felt the jet lag catching up with her again as Rick's deep English voice, sounding even more so in this land of different accents, laid out the first leg from Cairns to Port

Moresby, which would take them about two sailing days. The
boat bobbed rhythmically to the melody of a hundred loose
halyards clinking against their masts and she yawned.

It wasn't until a voice from outside disturbed them that
Stella realised two hours had passed in a drowsy haze and
she'd barely taken any of it in.

'Ahoy there! Anyone home?'

Rick frowned. 'Who's that?'

Stella's head cleared as she recognised the sultry tones
of the coffee-shop owner. 'I'm guessing it's the leggy, red-
headed cougar.'

Rick laughed as he took a swig of his second beer. 'Really?
Oh…'

He seemed disappointed, which perversely made her both
happy and annoyed and a lot more awake. 'Er…you invited
her here. What did you expect?'

'Did I?' Rick frowned. He didn't recall.

Stella blinked. 'You said, you should drop by the marina.
Women are literal creatures, Rick.'

He stood. 'That's cool.' He disappeared into the galley and
came out with another beer. 'It's never a hardship to spend
some time with a beautiful woman. Who appreciates a classic yacht.'

Stella rolled her eyes. 'She's a decade older than you.'

He shrugged, then grinned at her as he cracked the tops
on the beers. 'So?' And then she watched him disappear up
the winding staircase.

Great.

What the hell was *she* supposed to do while he dallied
above deck with a woman about the same age as her mother
as if he were some young buck in need of sexual tutelage?

God, no, he wouldn't…surely he wouldn't have sex with
her up there where anyone could see him? Surely he'd at least
bring her to his cabin?

But then the thought of him bringing her down here was

confronting on other levels. Stella didn't want another woman below deck sullying all that it meant to her—to them.

God, would she be forced to listen to them rocking the bloody boat all night?

Would they be loud?

She didn't think that Rick would be a silent lover. She'd always imagined he'd be quite vocal in his appreciation of a woman.

Just like Vasco.

She could only pray the jet lag still tugging at the peripheries of her consciousness would sink her completely under in a deep sound-proof abyss.

Stella could hear their muffled voices above her and could feel herself getting madder with each passing minute. She tried to concentrate on the weather charts and tide times on the laptop in front of her, but her eyes felt too gritty. She even pulled out her father's research papers and tried to immerse herself in them, but she was just too damn tired and the redhead's deep throaty laugh was just too damn distracting.

She could feel herself getting more and more tense.

How dared he entertain a lady and expect her to just meld into the furniture, stay below deck and pretend she wasn't even here?

It might be his boat but she wasn't going to feel ignored or non-existent. He had his whole life to be with as many women as he liked. To flirt and indulge in whatever hedonistic lifestyle he wanted.

But for the next few weeks he was on this boat with *her* with a job to do and he could bloody well take a break from being Mr Irresistible and keep his head in the game.

Stella was pacing when he joined her five minutes later, aware on some peripheral level she wasn't feeling particularly rational. 'That was quick,' she said testily.

Rick shrugged. Danielle's company had been pleasant

enough but he didn't feel like entertaining tonight. There was a lot of planning to do and he was aware of Stella below deck.

'Big day tomorrow,' he said as he made a beeline for the galley, throwing the empty beer bottles in the bin under the sink.

'You should have brought her down here and shown her around. I bet she was dying to see below deck—a woman with an eye for a classic yacht and all,' Stella said, sarcasm oozing from her pores.

Rick grinned as he washed his hands at the sink. 'Oh, she wanted to. But I told her you had a headache. You know, from the jet lag.'

'How considerate,' she said sweetly. 'She must have been devastated.'

'Nah...I don't really think she was *that* interested in the boat.'

Stella snorted. 'You don't say.'

Rick poked his head out of the galley to look at her. She seemed mad. 'You're bitchy when you're jet-lagged.'

'Yeh, headaches bring out the bitch in me too,' she snapped.

Rick saw a spark of heat turn her olive gaze to an ominous green, like a hailstorm. He knew he was in trouble, he just wasn't sure why. 'What's wrong?' he asked warily, approaching her.

Stella wasn't exactly sure why she was *so* mad all of a sudden, but she knew she was. She shook her head at him. 'You.'

'Okay...?'

'You honestly can't switch it off, can you?'

Rick frowned. 'Switch what off?'

'God, you should come with a flirt alert. How on earth are you possibly going to manage this trip, four bloody weeks, without a woman around to charm?'

Rick, who was used to spending lengthy periods at sea, wasn't worried about it. 'I think I'll manage,' he said dryly.

'Manage?' Stella snorted again. 'You can't go a day without trying to hook up.'

Rick laughed. 'I think you're exaggerating a little.'

Stella stopped pacing and glared at him. 'In thirty-six hours you have flirted with every woman who has crossed your path. Diana, the rental-car woman, the airline check-in chicky, the grandmother who ran the refreshment stall at Heathrow, several air stewardesses, the taxi driver, every waitress in the coffee shop today...'

She ticked off each conquest on a finger. 'And when we get on that boat tomorrow after about twelve hours you're going to start in on me *because you can't help yourself*,' she finished a little shrilly.

Rick blinked. Stel wasn't usually the nagging, hysterical type so it was either jet lag or PMS. Neither of which he was game to suggest, but he hoped it was the former because that surely couldn't last more than another day.

'But I always flirt with you.' He shrugged. 'It doesn't mean anything.'

Stella glared. 'Why the hell not?' she demanded, uncaring that she knew. 'Is there something wrong with me?'

Rick blinked, not quite able to believe he was having this conversation. 'That's not what I meant. There's nothing wrong with you. You're perfectly...' He groped around for a word that was flattering without saying all the things he'd desperately tried not to think about her over the years—curvy, sweet, bootylicious.

A Nathan-approved word.

'Decent.'

Decent?

Good God, she sounded as if she were someone's homely cousin who was all right at a pinch but was hardly likely to be picked to play spin the bottle at a party. Stella doubted she'd ever felt so underwhelmed in her life.

'Gee, thanks,' she snapped.

Rick pushed his hair off his face as he tried to comprehend how this night had gone so rapidly to hell. 'I don't understand… Do you…want me to mean it?' he asked.

Stella's breath hitched in her throat at the illicitness of the suggestion. What would *that* be like? To have all that deliberate blue-eyed charm turned on her? Like when they'd been teenagers and their banter had occasionally wandered into dangerous territory.

But grown up.

Diana's *you should have sex with him* slithered into her brain and she pushed it away.

'Of course I don't!' she said in her very best English-teacher-talking-to-a-student-with-a-crush voice. 'But I don't want you flirting with every other woman you come across either. It really is rather tiresome to watch and completely unproductive.'

Rick cocked an eyebrow. *He'd personally never found flirting to be unproductive.* But she was obviously accusing him of lack of control. 'You think I can't go a few lousy weeks without flirting with a woman?'

Stella crossed her arms. 'Oh, I'm sure of it.'

'Is this a dare?' he asked.

Stella felt the conversation suddenly shift gears. It should have taken her back to their childhood but the silk in his voice took her to another place entirely.

A very adult place.

'Sure.' She shrugged. 'I dare you. I dare you to go through this whole voyage without flirting with a single woman you meet along the way.'

Rick grinned, his gaze locking with hers. 'And what do I get?' he asked, his voice low.

The timbre of his voice stroked along all her tired nerve endings as he stared at her with his Vasco eyes.

What did he want?

Stella swallowed. 'Get?'

Rick held her gaze. 'If I win?'

Stella was lost for words for a moment. They'd never played for stakes before. Several inappropriate suggestions rose to mind but she quashed each one. She was too strung out to play games with him. 'How about my undying gratitude?' she quipped.

Rick shook his head slowly, dropping his gaze to her mouth. 'How about that kiss that we didn't quite get round to?'

Stella blinked as the teenage bad-boy looked back at her. It was a tantalising offer. One she knew he didn't expect her to take. But she'd never been one to back down from a dare and, frankly, the idea was as thrilling as it was illicit.

She smiled. 'Deal.' She held out her hand. He wouldn't be able to manage it, of course, but if the stakes were…interesting…maybe he'd at least try and comply.

Their gazes locked and Rick swallowed as he took her hand, cementing the deal.

Would she taste like coconuts too?

They cast off the next morning at eight o'clock, a good wind aiding their departure. The long-range weather forecast was favourable and Stella was feeling as if her body clock was finally back in sync.

Of course, she was also really embarrassed by her carry-on last night. She tried to apologise to Rick once they were out of the harbour and heading north.

'Are you trying to welch on the deal?' Rick teased. 'Because you know how much I love a challenge.'

She did. God knew how many times she'd come close to drowning while challenging him to a competition to see who could hold their breath underwater the longest.

He'd beat her every time.

Except for that time he'd let her win and she'd been so mad at him he'd promised never to do it again.

'Absolutely not,' she said, shaking her head. 'I stand by it.'

'Good.' He grinned. 'Now go write something.'

And she did. Sitting in a special chair at the bow of the boat, sun on her shoulders, breeze in her hair, laptop balanced on her knees, she found Lucinda flowed from her fingers onto the page. It was as if she frolicked and danced along the keys, slipping magically between Stella's fingers, informing every letter, controlling every mouse click.

The cursor no longer blinked at Stella from a blank page. Instead words, lovely rich words of a bygone era, filled all the white spaces up. When Rick brought her a snack and her hat she realised she'd been writing for two hours solid and the number down the bottom of the page told her she'd written thirteen hundred words.

Thirteen hundred glorious words.

The morning flowed into the afternoon; the perfect calm conditions continued. Rick occasionally called to her, pointing out a pod of dolphins or an island in the distance. She got up and stretched regularly and when she was grappling with a scene she'd take the wheel for a while and magically, like tankers on the horizon, the solution appeared.

By the end of the day she'd written three thousand words and she felt utterly exhilarated. And it wasn't all about the writing.

She'd forgotten how elemental sailing made a person feel. How it connected you to the earth on such a primitive level. How the feel of the waves beneath your feet and the push and pull of the tide drew you into the circadian rhythm of the planet.

How it connected her to her father.

She'd missed Nathan terribly the last six months, but out here he was everywhere. Every turn of the wheel, every flap of the sail, every pitch and roll of the hull.

They anchored just before sundown in the middle of nowhere. Just her and Rick bobbing in the middle of an enormous ocean beneath a giant dome blushing velvet and dappled with tangerine clouds.

Rick grilled steaks this time and Stella was pleased she'd kept a serving out of the freezer. She loved fish, but she knew by the time the voyage was over she'd be all fished out. And with three thousand words to celebrate, nice thick juicy steaks seemed like the perfect food. She tossed a salad and completed the meal with melt-in-your-mouth bread rolls.

It was utterly delicious and they savoured every morsel of the fresh food. Much later in their journey, when their fresh food had run out, the meals wouldn't be this exciting.

Of course, there would always be fish.

Stella took their plates while Rick cleaned the grill and she joined him on deck twenty minutes later after a quick shower. He was lying as he had the night before, flat on his back, stretched out beneath a vast canopy of black and silver.

Although tonight, at least, he'd decided to wear a shirt.

'Are we going to do this every night?' she asked, joining him.

He looked up at her. She was wearing a sarong tied around her neck in some fashion, the corners flapping in the breeze to show a little bare thigh. He looked back at the sky.

'Weather permitting,' he murmured.

Stella settled back, the slap of the halyard against the mast making a delightful clink. The stars seemed so close this far away from the light pollution of land.

'Well, I think I did very well today,' he said after they'd lain in companionable silence for a few minutes. 'Are you ready to concede yet?'

Stella laughed. 'There's only been me here.'

He smiled into the night. 'It won't make a difference.'

'Well, we'll see how it is when you're surrounded by all those Micronesian babes who want to be your own private deckhands.'

He chuckled then and Stella shivered as the delicious noise

slipped down her spine like a feather stroke. She raised her hand to distract herself, just as she had as a child, holding up her thumb to the moon and squinting, obliterating the glowing white orb from her vision.

She dropped her hand. 'They look like you could just pluck them from the sky, one by one, don't they?'

'And that's why you write romance novels,' Rick teased, rolling his head to the side to look at her.

Stella smiled and just as abruptly stopped. Rick seemed so laid-back about what she did.

He frowned. 'What's wrong?'

'Nothing,' she sighed.

'That's kind of a big sigh to be nothing. I thought you were ecstatic about your word count today.'

Stella let her head roll so she was facing him too. 'I am, I'm…beyond ecstatic. I'm just…'

'Just? Are you not happy with what you do?'

'No. I'm very happy with it. Especially now I have words,' she joked. 'I have a great publisher. An editor who's a saint, an agent who's a shark…'

'But?' he asked as she turned her head away to look at the sky. 'You should be proud of what you do. Nathan was. We're all so proud of you, Stel.'

Stella gave a light snort. 'Trust me, not everyone is so… proud of what I do.'

Rick frowned. 'Oh? Someone in particular?'

She looked at him again. 'Dale. He…broke off the engagement when he realised what I wrote.'

Nathan had told Rick about the break-up when it had occurred. Rick hadn't asked why, he'd just assumed it was the usual sort of stuff that broke relationships up. He did remember Nathan being secretly pleased. He'd always thought his daughter's long-term fiancé was a bit of a cold fish.

Rick had to admit to feeling a little pleased himself. He'd

never met Dale but Nathan's instincts about men had usually been spot on.

'He didn't know?'

She shook her head. 'Dale thought I was writing respected historical research on eighteenth-century pirates.'

Rick was confused. 'Didn't you tell him?'

'Of course I did, but he was never good at listening. He's an academic, one of those absent-minded professor types, and all he heard was historical and pirate…'

Rick suppressed a shudder. *He sounded like a total bore.*

'So,' he said, wanting to clarify the situation before he spoke ill of her idiot ex, 'he dumped you when he found out you wrote…'

Stella nodded. 'Trashy, smutty, dirty little books.'

Rick cocked an eyebrow. *He really had to read that book.* 'You write trashy smut?' What the hell was wrong with the man? Didn't he realise that was a really good reason to hang onto a woman?

Stella rolled her eyes. 'No. I write historical romantic fiction for women. Dale called them trashy and smutty.'

Rick sucked in a breath. *What a dufus.* 'How did he find out?'

'One of his students asked him if he was the inspiration for Vasco Ramirez.'

Rick rolled up onto his elbow and looked down at her. 'Was he?'

Stella laughed then. The irony of Rick, Vasco Ramirez personified, asking that question was just too much. 'Most definitely not.'

Rick grinned. 'Ouch.'

Stella felt instantly contrite—not everyone looked like an eighteenth-century pirate. 'No, I'm sorry, I didn't mean it like that. Dale's lovely…was lovely. In kind of a…self-absorbed way. He's just not…buccaneer material.'

'Well,' Rick announced. 'The man's clearly an idiot.'

'Not really…he has an IQ in the hundred and thirties.'

Rick fell back against the deck. 'He can't be too smart if his fiancée is writing smutty novels and he doesn't use that to his advantage.'

Stella burst out laughing. 'His advantage? How?'

Rick shrugged. 'Dress up in breeches and make you read it aloud to him.'

Stella laughed again. The very thought was as wicked as it was absurd. Dale would no sooner have done that than flown to the moon. 'Dale was a little too strait-laced for role playing. In fact I think he considered human desire a little beneath him altogether. Too…messy or something.'

There was just something about laughing with Rick in the night under the stars that encouraged confidences and she felt as if they were kids again, whispering their secrets to each other.

Rick couldn't believe what he was hearing. In fact he was pretty damn sure he didn't want to hear it. And not just because a woman like Stella, or any woman for that matter, should not be having mediocre sex. But because putting sex and Stella in the same sentence was something he'd avoided his entire life.

'Why on earth did you stay with him?' he asked.

Stella rolled her head to face him. That one was easy.

'Because he was a nice guy. A good guy. A kind guy. He made me laugh.' *Not in the ribald way Rick made her laugh but in a lovely, easy way that warmed her up inside.* 'He had a great job. On terra firma. He wanted to get married. He wanted kids.'

Rick almost yawned, it sounded so boring, but the way her voice softened was telling. He looked away. How could someone who had the swell of oceans running in her veins settle for such mediocrity?

'Well, it sounds like you're well shot of him to me,' he said after a few moments star gazing. 'A woman who writes smut needs someone to inspire her.'

Stella laughed. 'You're incorrigible.'

'That's what you like about me.'

She thumped him on the chest. Yeh, it *was* what she liked about him but she wasn't going to admit it.

'I'm going to bed,' she said, sitting up.

He sat also. 'I'm up for that.'

Stella looked behind her at his bad-boy grin and rolled her eyes. 'By myself.'

'I can do smut.'

Stella laughed. 'I bet you can.'

He held up his hand. 'Just saying. The offer's out there.'

Stella shook her head. 'I think this is called flirting, Rick.'

'Hey, you said, with women I meet along the way. I already know you. You're fair game.'

Stella guessed she'd walked right into that one.

'Besides I gotta put the flirt somewhere. It's not good to let it build up. Men,' he said, lowering his voice, 'should never let anything build up.'

Lucky for her she was used to Rick's teasing and was sufficiently over the jet lag to not let it push her buttons. She stood. 'Goodnight, Rick.'

'Sleep tight.' He grinned as he watched her walk away.

Then there were just the stars, the ocean and him, but not even they could keep him from the smutty book he had secreted in his cabin.

He gave her five minutes, then followed her down.

Six hours later, Rick read *The End* and knew he would never be the same again. Diana had been right. It was most illuminating. The hard-on he'd got in chapter two was still there and there was no way it was going away unless he did something about it.

Fortunately now he had plenty of images to help him in that department.

Two things were crystal clear.

Number one—Dale was an idiot of the first order. Hell, if he had a woman that had this sort of stuff in her head— the sheer eroticism of the beautifully scripted love scenes still clung to his loins—he wouldn't let her out of his bed let alone his life.

Number two—the most shocking of all.

She'd written the book about him.

He was Vasco Ramirez.

CHAPTER FIVE

Lady Mary stifled a gasp as Captain Ramirez rose from the tin bath tub with the fluid grace of a stallion. Water sluiced down the long lines of his body as the flickering lamplight gilded his bronzed skin, throwing it both into mysterious shadow and enticing relief.

The mucous membranes of her throat cracked as dry as parchment, her heart skipped frantically in her chest.

She should not be here.

She should not be spying on a man, a nude man, who was unaware of being watched.

But she simply could not stop.

The last time she'd seen flesh this magnificent had been at Lord Ladbrooke's stables and her nostrils flared as she remembered how all that leashed power had felt beneath her jodhpurs as she'd straddled and then ridden the Arabian beauty bareback.

Much to her aunt's chagrin.

Lord alone knew what she'd do now witnessing Mary's scandalous behaviour. There'd be smelling salts for sure.

But, alas, Mary could not take her eyes off the man.

Steam still rose in wisps around his calves as he stood waiting for the excess water to run off. She held her breath as her gaze roamed over the board-taut planes of his shoulders, obscured towards the middle by sleek wet strips of dark hair. Water trekked from the dripping ends and she followed the path of one errant droplet, gleaming in the light, as it slid down the furrow of his spine nestled between the well-defined muscles either side.

She lost it in shadow as it entered the dip of his back, bracketed by enticing hollows, but her eyes roamed south regardless to the rise of his buttocks. Two firm slabs of muscle, potently male even in his relaxed state, greeted her.

Her gaze was drawn to the left where an imperfection snagged her attention. There, in the centre of his left buttock, lay a large smooth brown birthmark.

It was utterly fascinating and Mary stared at it open-mouthed. It was a perfect circle as if some lover, for he looked to be a man who took lovers, had drawn it deliberately to brand him.

Mary's cheeks flamed at the risqué image and she felt the roughness of her breath as it quickened in her lungs.

Just when she thought he'd turned to stone he turned slightly, affording Mary a different view. Her gaze brushed along the flare of a bicep, the jut of a masculine hip, which seemed as savage as it did graceful, and the perfect delineation of a meaty quadricep that seemed to vibrate with barely leashed power.

And then there was his...

Mary swallowed. She had seen illustrations of the nude male anatomy in obscure texts in her uncle's library when she'd been fifteen but they hadn't managed to capture the sheer beauty of the real thing. The long elegant line of the male member in all its potency was a sight to behold.

It was more elongated and the girth more significant than she'd ever imagined. The curls at its base more enticing.

How magnificent would it look standing out proud as she'd seen on the midnight Arabian?

Mary felt a strange sensation take root deep inside her.

How on earth did it fit?

Captain Ramirez suddenly reached for a nearby towel, covering himself as he stepped out of the bath, his fascinating birthmark the last thing she saw before everything was obscured. Just as quickly he'd padded over to the door that led to his private bedchamber and disappeared through it.

Mary let out the breath she'd been holding. It stuttered noisily into the air around her. She knew she should move but she was utterly incapable.

Until now she'd assumed that pirates didn't bathe.

She would be grateful until the day she died that Captain Vasco Ramirez had shattered that rather high-handed illusion.

Vasco was breathing rather heavily himself as he shut the door to his bedchamber, leaning against it, his long sable lashes covering the smoulder in his devil blue eyes. Ever since he'd seen Lady Mary in the looking glass peeking out from behind the curtains he'd been determined to shock her.

But he hadn't been prepared for her thorough appreciation. Nor for his completely involuntary reaction to her fascinated scrutiny.

His fancy did not usually involve gently bred ladies but he'd seen those flared nostrils, heard that muffled gasp.

Maybe beneath all those prim petticoats and haughty eyes beat a passionate heart. Maybe she wasn't as indifferent to him as her demeanour suggested.

Maybe she could be persuaded to make this voyage a lot more bearable for both of them?

Rⁱᶜᵏ shut the book as he finished chapter two.

Again.

He could hear Stella moving around above him and knew he had to get out of bed and get under way but he wasn't sure he could look her in the eye this morning.

And—he looked down at the tented sheet—he needed a little time to compose himself...

He ran his fingers over the glossy cover of *Pleasure Hunt*, the metallic letters boldly pronouncing her name—*Stella Mills*.

This *was not* the Stella Mills he knew.

What on earth had happened to her? The Stella who had played mermaid and pirates? Who liked to snorkel and scuba dive? Who liked to read and watch the stars at night? The Stella who hated carrots and could almost hold her breath as long as he could?

The one who had been devastated when her parents had divorced and had made him promise that whatever happened in their lives they would always be friends.

Of course that Stella had been ten years old.

Just the way he liked her.

Because otherwise he had to think of her as a very different Stella.

A grown-up Stella. Who got engaged.

Who had sex.

Who was twenty-seven and *not* the virgin her father had hoped she would be for ever.

Not if *Pleasure Hunt* was anything to go by anyway.

God, she probably didn't even hate carrots any more.

Rick threw the covers off. This was ridiculous. And not helping his situation down below.

He cut straight to the crux of the issue, or one aspect of it anyway.

She *was not* Lady Mary.

He let it reverberate around his head for good measure.

Lady Mary was a character she'd made up. In that vivid, hot, lustrous, dirty—*God, so dirty*—imagination of hers.

Just because Vasco was him, didn't mean that Lady Mary was her.

It didn't mean she'd been fantasising about him sexually. Or that she'd put herself into a character whose lust for his character bordered on pornographic obsession.

That was just plain crazy.

There was nothing remotely similar about Lady Mary and Stella—nothing.

So he needed to get over himself.

He needed to go and take a shower—a cold one—and get the bloody boat moving.

He was on deck twenty minutes later. And he was in big, big trouble. Suddenly the filter that had always been in place where she was concerned had been stripped away. Those teenage dreams he'd had about her and refused to let himself dwell upon were front and centre.

She was in teeny tiny denim shorts with a frayed edge and a shirt that barely met in the middle. A straw cowboy-style hat, the edges curled up, sat low over her eyes and held her tucked-up hair in place save for a few haphazard wisps that had escaped and brushed her nape.

The girl he always saw, the one he'd trained himself to see, ever since Nathan had sprung them about to kiss, was gone for ever.

Now he saw the ripe bulge of her breasts as the bra he could clearly see through the thin fabric of her shirt pushed and lifted in all the right ways. The wink of her belly button taunting him from the strip of bare skin at her midriff. The killer curve where her hip flared from the tiny line of her waist.

He'd never noticed how curvy she was before. Not consciously anyway. Consciously he'd always thought of her as short and cute.

Like an elf or maybe a munchkin.

But there was nothing cute about those curves—they should come with a yellow warning sign.

And he was stuck on board with them for the next few weeks.

'Well, about time,' Stella said as she caught Rick's advance in her peripheral vision. 'Another gorgeous day for sailing.'

Rick smiled, his gaze drawn to her mouth. The mouth that was nowhere near as innocent as he'd always thought. A mouth he tried and failed not to think about on his body the way Lady Mary's had been on Vasco's.

Stella popped the lid on a bottle of sunscreen and squirted some into her palm. 'If you get us under way,' she said, slapping it on her chest, 'I'll cook some bacon and eggs.'

Rick swallowed as Stella distributed the white liquid to her shoulders and upper arms and across the swell of her cleavage, dipping her fingers beneath the fabric a little.

Do not look at her breasts. Do not *look at her breasts.*

Too late.

He looked at her breasts.

'Sure,' he said distractedly as her hands continued to massage the crème until her cleavage glistened in the sun.

Stella frowned at him as he stood there looking at her. Was he…was he perving at her chest? There were times when they'd been younger, pre her sweet-sixteen debacle, when she'd caught him looking at her, when their gazes had locked and he'd smile at her with wolfish appreciation, but that had been a long time ago.

'Rick?'

Her voice brought him back from the fantasy of licking every inch of the crème off her. He blinked and quickly donned his sunglasses. 'Yes, absolutely, getting under way.' He saluted, turning from her gratefully, his hands trembling as if he were fifteen years old again and trying to undo Sharon Morgan's bra.

He really needed to get a grip.

By the time the sun was high in the sky Rick was half-way to crazy. The boat was travelling along at a steady clip, which left him nothing else to do other than stare at Stella. Even metres away from him in her low chair, doing nothing but writing, she destroyed his concentration. She was almost directly in his line of sight, her legs supporting her laptop, her shirt riding up her spine to reveal a good portion of skin, including the dimples at the small of her back.

With conversation non-existent, he was left with a lot of time to think. A lot of time for his mind to wander.

Standing at the helm, the wheel in his hand, the ocean at his command, it was a little hard not to think of himself as the all-conquering pirate Vasco Ramirez.

The Vasco who decided to turn his treasure hunt into a pleasure hunt. Who actively seduced Lady Mary after the bath scene and whose slow, deliberate dance with her was both clever and cunning.

Rick's mind wandered to those scenes of calculated seduction. Vasco washing Mary's hair on deck. Vasco removing a splinter from her finger with his teeth. Vasco cutting into the juicy flesh of a dripping pear with his jewelled dagger and feeding her slice after slice.

And the sexiest scene of all where Vasco had tied her spreadeagled in her under-things to his bed until Mary had admitted her desire for him.

That one had got Rick hotter than a summer day on the equator.

In fact just thinking about it now was getting him pretty damn hot. Not helped by the fact that she had abandoned her seated position and was doing a sexy little stretch, bending over and touching her toes, then arching her back as she linked her hands above her head and twisted from side to side.

Oh, Lord, kill me now.

She turned then and walked towards him and he was

pleased, as her breasts jiggled enticingly, for the secure place-
ment of his very dark sunglasses.

'You fancy a cold beer and a bite to eat?' Stella asked as
she approached.

'Sounds great,' he said.

Stella patted him absently on the arm. 'Be right back,'
she said.

Rick stayed very still as the fleeting touch seemed to reach
deep down inside and stroke something that it just shouldn't
have. Since when had a perfunctory touch from her had such
an effect? But he suddenly understood Ramirez's puzzlement
over the sensations that Lady Mary had created when she'd
clung to his sleeve briefly during some choppy weather.

Rick shook his head at the direction of his errant thoughts.
Bloody hell, had he been emasculated overnight?

When Stella rejoined him ten minutes later with some ham
and salad rolls and two beers, he'd found his testicles and got
over himself.

'Put it on autopilot,' Stella said, pressing the beer into his
hand. 'Come and sit with me.'

Yeh, that was just what he needed.

But he did it anyway.

'So, how's the book going?' he asked, nodding at the shut
laptop as he took a man-sized swallow of beer to dilute the
absolute unmanly curiosity over her current romance novel.

Stella nodded. 'Coming along very nicely. I'm just about
finished with the first chapter. I've emailed Diana—she's ecstatic. I think Joy had threatened her with editing non-fic if I
didn't deliver.' Stella grinned.

Rick smiled too. She seemed relaxed and willing to chat
about the book. Maybe, instead of wondering whether Lady
Mary was her, which was, quite frankly, driving him nuts, he
could just come out and ask. Or at least start a conversation
where he could work his way round to it.

'So, what's the book about?' he asked as he took a bite out of his bread roll.

Stella looked up at him from under the brim of her hat. 'You really want to know?'

Rick stopped chewing. 'Of course, why wouldn't I?'

Stella blinked. For as long as she'd known him Rick's tastes had run to non-fiction books on anything to do with the salvage industry and shipwrecks. And *Phantom* comics.

'It's not really your thing.'

Oh, if only she knew how suddenly it was exactly his thing. He looked at her. 'It's yours. I'm interested.'

Stella stared at him for a moment, taken aback by his sincerity. 'Good answer.' She smiled.

He smiled back. She looked so damn sweet, how could she have such a dirty mind? 'So?' He quirked an eyebrow.

She didn't know where to start. She wasn't used to sharing this sort of information with anyone. Only Diana had known about *Pleasure Hunt* and even then Stella had been reticent to share any of the details in the early stages of the book. Non-writers didn't understand how storylines and characters weren't always crystal clear and well defined.

'It's about a mermaid,' she said. 'Called Lucinda.'

And then for some strange reason, under his scrutiny, she blushed. She thought about all the times they'd played pirate and mermaid as kids, swimming through the tropical waters of wherever they happened to be at the time.

'You know I've always had a thing for mermaids,' she said defensively.

Rick's gaze locked with hers. 'I do.'

Stella shrugged. 'She came to me in a dream.'

He nodded, wishing he'd been privy to that dream. Hell, if her dream life was as rich as her on-page fantasy life he wished he were privy to all of them.

'And the hero?' he asked.

Something held Stella back. She straightened the hat on

her head, then whisked it off and let her hair tumble down, stalling for time as she looked towards the horizon. 'I don't know much about the hero this time,' she said with what she hoped seemed like artistic vagueness.

Rick followed the stream of her hair as the stiffening ocean breeze blew it behind her. His palm itched to tangle in it and he kept it firmly planted around his beer. 'Is that unusual?' he asked.

'I don't know. I'm new to this and it's just the way it's happened.'

Rick slid a sideways glance at her. 'Did that happen with your first hero?'

Stella's heart skipped a beat as she glanced at him. 'No,' she said casually. 'He came to me…fairly well developed.'

Rick bit back a smile. *Hell, yeah, honey, no prizes for guessing why.* 'Does he have a name at least, this new guy?'

Stella blushed again. 'Inigo.'

Rick smiled. 'Ah…good choice.'

Stella looked at him and returned his smile grudgingly. 'Thank you.' It was surprisingly hard to talk about the hero with Rick and his Vasco Ramirez eyes staring straight at her even from behind his midnight shades.

Rick knew he had a good opening but was surprised by the pound of his heart as he contemplated the question.

Did he really want to know the answer?

He forced himself to take up inspection of the horizon so the question would seem casual rather than targeted. 'Do you base any of your characters on people you know?' he asked casually.

Stella glanced at him sharply. Did he know? Had he read *Pleasure Hunt*? She'd sent a copy to the *Persephone* for her father, which Rick could have got his hands on, she supposed, but it had been in a box of things that had been cleared from his cabin and sent to her after his death still in pristine condition.

The spine hadn't been cracked and it had been obvious to her that it had been unread.

It was an innocent enough question on the surface—one she'd been asked a hundred times by fans and media alike—but her shoulders tensed as she inspected that inscrutable profile just in case.

He seemed his usual relaxed self, soaking up some rays and downing a beer with the unconscious grace of an Old Spice model.

Besides, she doubted there would be any way he would have read it and not realised immediately who Vasco was. And she knew Rick well enough to know that he wouldn't have been able to resist taunting her mercilessly about it.

'No,' she said faintly, hoping her voice sounded stronger than it felt.

Rick stifled a chuckle. *Liar.* For damn sure Vasco Ramirez was him.

'So they just come to you…like in a dream or something…?' he asked innocently.

'Something like that,' she said vaguely. 'Although if I'm to be honest,' she admitted, trying to divert his attention off the hero, 'I suppose that the heroine is me.'

Rick coughed noisily as he inhaled some of his beer into his windpipe, necessitating her to beat him on the back a few times. He gasped and wheezed and coughed while his airway cleared the irritant.

Vasco probably never did anything so undignified.

'So,' he clarified once he could speak again, 'the heroines are…you?'

Please say no. Please don't let me have to imagine that Lady Mary is really you.

Damn it. He should have left it alone.

Stella blushed as Lady Mary filled her vision. 'Well, to a degree, I suppose, yes. I'm a woman so I can write a female character from my own experiences. In that respect, in very generic terms, I guess they are.'

Rick breathed easier. She was talking in generalisations. Not specifics. 'So Lucinda isn't you?'

Stella shook her head. 'Well, she's more me than Lady Mary,' she admitted.

Rick felt the tension ooze away completely.

Hah! There. She wasn't Lady Mary.

Phew.

'Lady Mary's from the first book?' he asked innocently.

Stella nodded as her embarrassment slipped away. It was actually quite good thinking this sort of stuff out loud. Knowing the differences could only help with her writing process.

Maybe Rick was a good sounding board?

'Lucinda has a strength of character that Lady Mary didn't. She's not waiting around to be rescued—in fact, she's going to rescue the hero, who's being held in chains.'

Rick tried not to think about how that scene would pan out. 'And Lady Mary is weak?'

Because he'd thought, in her own way, Mary had a startling resilience.

Stella shook her head. 'No, she's not weak, she's just more passive. But that's really just a product of the times and her upper-class background.'

Rick thought of the scene where Mary had finally succumbed to Vasco's seduction. There had been nothing passive about her then. And nothing passive about the way she'd totally turned the emotional tables on him.

'Definitely not you, then,' he smiled, relieved.

Stella smiled back. *If only he knew.* Beneath Lady Mary's petticoats and pantaloons lay Stella's every secret desire. She drained her beer, then checked her watch. 'Right, enough time skiving off. Lucinda is whispering sweet nothings in my head.'

Rick frowned. 'They talk to you?'

'Oh, yes.' Stella nodded. 'Most insistently usually.'

He swallowed. 'The heroes as well as the heroines?'

'Yep.'

Rick's mind boggled. 'What do they say?'

Stella shrugged. 'Their thoughts, dreams, desires.'

Good God—had Lady Mary whispered those things to Stella? Had she told Stella she wanted to see Vasco naked in the bath, that she wanted him to suck her finger into his mouth and she wanted to be tied to his bed?

Or had it been Vasco telling Stella what *he* wanted to do to Mary? Describing it in all the erotic detail that it had appeared in the book?

Had Stella been hearing him in her head?

Rick had never been so happy to see terra firma in all his life when they spotted the Papua New Guinea mainland mid-afternoon. His attempt to dissipate the heat of his thoughts hadn't exactly gone to plan and he was pleased to be getting off the boat and distracting himself for a while.

They motored into Port Moresby harbour and docked at the Royal Papua Yacht Club. After seeing to all the official formalities they headed for the club.

'Remember,' Stella said as Rick smiled at a beautiful dark-skinned woman who openly ogled him as she passed by, 'you're on a dare.'

Rick almost groaned out loud. If he had to share quarters with a woman who wrote sexy literature for a living and dressed in next to nothing, then it was vital to put his flirt somewhere!

The fact that he was now bound to a ridiculous dare was just the really rotten icing on a really sucky cake. What was the world coming to when he couldn't negate some totally inappropriate sexual urges with some harmless flirting?

He smiled at her. 'Piece of cake.'

Stella grinned as she fell in beside him. She was so going to enjoy this!

He tried to ditch her first thing in the cool, modern surrounds of the yacht club, but there was no way she was letting him walk around unaccompanied, flirting with no redress. She stuck to him like glue as he organised refuelling and restocking of their fresh food supplies and some onwards paperwork for their visit to Micronesia.

They found a nearby craft market and she watched him get crankier as they moved through the stalls thronging with colour and spice and wall-to-wall gorgeous local women. She asked him his opinion about earrings, bikinis and having her hair plaited. None of which he had a strong opinion on other than exasperation.

She bought a sarong and an anklet that had a tiny shell and a little bell on a piece of rope. It was nautical and she was thrilled with her purchase.

He was plain annoyed.

By the time they'd returned to the boat after an evening meal at the club, he was withdrawn and every inch the brooding pirate.

Due to cloud cover and lack of interest there was no star gazing tonight. Just a strictly professional conversation about their onward leg and a discussion revolving around the weather, which wasn't looking good for the next couple of days, but the long-range forecast remained excellent considering they were in the monsoon season.

'You okay?' she asked innocently as she picked up their empty coffee mugs and padded barefoot towards the galley. 'You seem kind of tense?'

Honestly, the man didn't realise how much his very survival depended on his banter with women—he needed it as if it were oxygen.

'The no flirting getting to you?' she queried, suppressing the humour that bubbled in her chest.

Rick heard the laughter in her voice only on a peripheral level as the tinkle of her anklet obliterated all else.

Great.

As if he weren't conscious enough already of her every movement, he was going to *hear* her every movement as well.

He'd probably hear her at night rolling over in bed.

He plastered a smile to his face. 'I'm fine,' he said. It had only been forty-eight hours, for crying out loud—just how oversexed did she think he was? 'I'm going up on deck to plot the course into the sat nav.'

Stella smiled as he departed. She had this dare nailed.

CHAPTER SIX

ON DECK the humid night was quiet and still, clouds obscuring what would almost be a full moon. Not even a light breeze tinkled the halyards. Faint music drifted down from the yacht club but the moorings were otherwise peaceful. No boats had cabin lights on, no one walked about stopping to chat, no low muffled conversations could be heard.

No one around to witness Rick gently belting his head against the wheel.

When he'd embarked on this voyage everything had been clear cut. *The Mermaid* and Inigo's treasure lay out there somewhere and he and his good friend Stella, *whom he'd known for ever, who despite some disturbing dreams was like a sister to him*, were going to find it.

After all, it was what Nathan had wanted.

Now he had a whole other picture going on in his head and he was damn sure there was nothing brotherly about it.

And definitely *not* what Nathan had wanted.

Nathan hadn't told Rick to leave Stella alone that day he'd caught them almost kissing. But he *had* spoken about how special his daughter was and left Rick in no doubt that he'd wanted someone just as special for Stella. Certainly a bunch of transient deckhands and divers on a motley collection of salvage boats had not measured up to Nathan's expectations in any way, shape or form.

Nathan had wanted for his daughter the one thing he'd never been able to give his own wife—stability.

Someone who was going to be there for her always.

And Nathan had made sure every man in his employ had known that his daughter was off-limits.

Himself included.

But that was then. And this was now.

Nathan was dead. And Stella was all grown up.

She had breasts and hips and an imagination that would make a sailor blush.

How on earth was he supposed to ignore that? Particularly when she was downstairs right now—he could hear that bloody bell all the way up here—prancing around, enjoying herself, feeling all smug at his expense.

And it was only day two.

How nuts would he be by the end of it all?

Hell, how nuts would he be in a week?

Unless…

Rick pulled his head off the steering wheel as the cunning of a certain pirate came to his rescue. He sat ramrod straight.

What if he took control of the situation? Turned the tables on her a little?

What if he were to take some of those tantalising scenes from *Pleasure Hunt* and give them life? He'd already established that she wasn't included in their little dare. Maybe he could have some more fun…

Vasco Ramirez had been determined to make the voyage with Lady Mary a pleasure hunt—maybe he should too?

Of course he'd never step over the line, the bondage scene would have to go begging, but what fun it could be seeing if he could get Stella all het up. After all, those scenes were written by her about him. Maybe he could indulge those fantasies for her just a little, give her a taste of the real thing?

It would be fun to see how she reacted.

Would she guess what he was doing or would she be unaware? Would she reject his boundary pushing or would she embrace it with the abandon with which she'd scribed it?

His gaze fell on the shower at the stern of the boat and he smiled.

Stella was putting the supplies away in the galley when she heard a loud splash outside the porthole in front of her. She frowned as she peered out into the night.

Maybe Rick had thrown himself overboard, the dare just too much?

'Rick?' she called, a smile on her face. No answer. 'Rick?' Still no answer.

Maybe it was one of Moresby's infamous rascals trying to steal from them and he'd knocked Rick unconscious and into the water.

Her smile died as her heart started hammering in her chest. She reached for the nearest weapon, a heavy-based fry pan, and decided to go up and investigate. She climbed the spiral staircase, one tread at a time, an itch up her spine.

She took a deep breath, then popped her head above the deck line, like a meerkat.

'Rick?' she whispered while her eyes took a second or two to adjust from the bright light below to the low cloud-affected moonlight outside.

Still nothing.

She caught a slight movement towards the helm of the boat as the sound of running water defined itself from the gentle slap of sea against hull and the trilling of insects. She squinted to make out the shape, her vision slowly adjusting to its night capabilities.

It was a person…

A man.

Taking a shower.

Taking a shower?

The moon chose that moment to come out from behind the

scudding clouds that had been hampering its brilliance all night and Stella was afforded a side view of the man standing beneath the shower spray as if someone had switched on a spotlight.

Rick.

A one hundred per cent, buck naked, Rick.

She stood there frozen to the spot for a long moment caught between two impulses. To get out now before he discovered she was staring at his naked body or just stop and take in every magnificent inch.

As the celestial spotlight continued to bathe him in milky brilliance the latter won out.

The shower head was behind him, his head tipped back, his face raised to the night as the spray bathed his shoulder-length locks into a sleek, silky sheath. His eyes were shut as if worshipping the moonbeams that painted him in alabaster.

He looked like a statue. A Michelangelo nude.

With all the beautiful symmetry of fluid muscles and the more subtle details of sinews, tendons and veins in living, breathing relief.

Water sluiced over his broad shoulders, his chest, his biceps. It ran down the planes of his back, following the curve of his spine, dipping into those two sexy dimples above the rise of his buttocks. It flowed down firm flanks and rippled like a waterfall across the defined ridges of his abdomen.

Rivulets of water ran down one powerful thigh pressed slightly forward, the knee bent, obscuring her view any lower, and Stella frowned.

Damn it, so close...

Vasco's bath scene had been written over two years ago, and while a lot of it had been scripted out of her imagination some of it hadn't. Having grown up with Rick wearing barely anything at all—boardies or a skin-tight diving suit being his everyday attire—she'd had plenty of inspiration for Vasco's body and had been able to portray it with startling accuracy.

There had been some parts, however, that she'd had to... embellish.

It would be nice to know the truth of it. Had her fevered imaginings accurately represented *all* of Vasco or had it been pure whimsy on her behalf?

And then, as if he'd read her mind, he shifted, twisting his body slightly in her direction, straightening his bent knee and transferring his weight to his other thigh, and she no longer had to wonder if she'd got it right because the evidence that she had was right there.

Riccardo Granville was most definitely Vasco Ramirez in the flesh.

Rick turned so his back was to Stella and smiled to himself as he tilted his neck from side to side, letting the lukewarm water run over muscle that was surprisingly tense. The concentration it had taken to appear unselfconscious and relaxed, as if he were alone and being unwatched, had been much harder to carry off than he'd thought. But to see Stella's head pop up and then feel her avid gaze on him as tangible as the water cascading from the shower head had made the exercise worthwhile.

He was back in control again and that was exactly the way he liked it. Even if he was playing games with someone he had no business playing games with.

But if she was going to secretly put him in a book and not expect him to have a bit of fun with that then she'd completely forgotten about his devilish sense of humour.

As long as he kept it light and remembered who she was—Nathan's daughter, not a single, fully grown woman who wrote dirty books—and where the line was, it would work out just fine.

They'd both have a laugh at the end of the voyage and get on with their lives.

It was win-win as far as he was concerned.

* * *

The second Stella strained to see that birthmark she'd been fascinated with since she'd been five years old she knew that happenstance had turned into voyeurism. She forced herself to cease and desist. With one long last lingering look at possibly the most beautiful rear end in the world, certainly in historical romance fiction, she slunk back down below deck, fry pan still in hand.

She should feel guilty; she knew that. If the positions had been reversed she'd have been mortified. But strangely she didn't. No harm had been committed. He didn't know that she'd been watching him or that he'd just fulfilled a particularly potent fantasy of hers—so potent she'd put it in a book!—and she certainly wasn't going to tell him!

But she would use it.

Late at night when a day of crafting sensual tension or a torrid love scene left her restless and achy and the dictates of her body would not be ignored, a naked Rick bathed in shower spray and moonbeams would come in handy.

Very handy indeed.

Vasco examined the milky white perfection of Lady Mary's hand. He cradled it in the palm of his much bigger, much darker one and admired the contrast for a moment. This was what they'd look like in his bed, their limbs entwined, their stomachs pressed together—coconut and coffee.

He stroked his thumb down the length of her index finger where the long slither of wood had embedded itself and let it drift across her palm. He heard the slight intake of her breath and felt her resistance to his hold.

He looked up into her emerald eyes. 'It's not as bad as it looks,' he murmured.

Mary swallowed. They were seated, her knees primly together beneath her skirts, his legs spread wide in that lord-of-all-he-surveyed way of his, bracketing hers. The fabric of his breeches pulled taut across his thighs as he leaned in over her hand, his head perilously close to her cleavage.

'It really just needs a pair of tweezers,' she said, trying to pull her hand back. He resisted and she resigned herself to the unsettling heat of his touch.

Vasco smiled at her, her pink mouth a tempting bow before him. 'I think I can do better than that.'

His voice was low and silky and Mary felt it in places that she'd only recently, thanks to him, become aware of. Her green gaze locked with the startling blue of his as he raised her finger to his mouth and sucked it inside.

Vasco watched surprise pucker her mouth into a cute little O shape as her pupils dilated. Her breathing was loud in the space between them as she lowered her gaze to where his mouth tasted her. He felt a half-hearted attempt to pull away again but countered it by laving her finger with long strokes of his tongue.

Her whimper went straight to his groin.

Mary felt the throb ease as Vasco ministered to her wound in this most unusual fashion. Her gaze returned to his, finding him watching her with something in those mesmerising eyes she couldn't fathom. She didn't know what it was but she did know she'd seen it there before.

And it was both dangerous and enticing.

Still holding her gaze, Vasco slowly withdrew his lips, his teeth seeking and finding the rough end of the splinter burrowed in at the tip. He nipped at it until he held it firmly, then slowly eased it out, her glistening finger slipping from his mouth altogether. For a moment he held the liberated splinter between his teeth, then turned his head and spat it on the floor.

He smiled as he turned back to face her. 'That's better,' he murmured.

Mary couldn't move. Her finger or anything else for

that matter. She just sat there, hand still in his, finger moist from his ministrations, staring at his mouth. A mouth that had turned her insides to jelly.

'Th-thank you,' she stammered, belatedly remembering her manners.

Vasco lowered his head to her finger again, and pressed a gentle lingering kiss to the exit wound.

He grinned. 'My pleasure.'

Mary felt a sudden urge to call for smelling salts.

After a restless sleep Stella wasn't in any hurry to look Rick in the eye for the first time since her voyeurism of last night. She'd gone straight to her quarters after her little peeping Tom episode, thus avoiding him altogether.

But she couldn't stay in her cabin for ever and it wasn't as if he knew that she'd spied on him. All she had to do was not blush and stammer when she greeted him and pretty soon the awkwardness would pass.

The memory would be emblazoned on her frontal lobe for ever but the awkwardness would pass!

'Hey,' she said to Rick as she wandered into the galley fifteen minutes later. He was sitting at the dining table poring over charts. Fully clothed. She looked away as he looked up at her.

Rick forced himself not to smile like a Cheshire cat, but just give a normal everyday *hey* kind of a smile. Which was kind of difficult when greeted with another pair of brief shorts and some kind of strapless shirt, leaving her shoulders bare and her cleavage…enhanced.

'Morning,' he said. *You saucy little pervert in barely any clothes.* 'Sleep well?'

He assumed she'd had a pretty fitful sleep if that damn bell jingling was anything to go by.

Stella steeled herself to look at him again and gave a non-committal shrug. 'Fine,' she murmured.

Rick stifled a smile as she looked away. *Liar.* Good, now they were even. Between the damn book, that silly little bell and an array of teeny tiny clothes, sleep had become a rare commodity.

'You were in bed early last night,' he mused, because he just couldn't resist teasing her a little as she had done over their flirting bet last night. 'Everything okay?'

Stella's breath hitched as she popped two pieces of bread in the toaster. 'Fine,' she replied, her gaze planted firmly on the job at hand.

Rick suppressed a chuckle at her monosyllabic replies. He'd have loved to tease her some more, hell he could have done it all day, but the weather wasn't the best out there and they should be getting under way.

He picked up his plate and glass and headed towards the galley, squeezing behind her to get to the sink. He felt her stiffen a little as he caught a whiff of browning toast and coconut. Her hair sat in a messy ponytail on top of her head, leaving her neck exposed, and he had the craziest urge to slip his arms around her waist and nuzzle into it.

He stepped away from the temptation—teasing her was one thing, acting as if they'd set up house was another. He placed his plate in the sink and downed the last of his orange juice in one gulp. 'It's going to be a bit choppy out there today so I'll get us under way,' he said.

'Fine,' Stella said again, keeping rigidly still until he'd safely disappeared up the stairs. When the toast popped thirty seconds later she realised she'd been staring out of the port-hole thinking about him naked.

Oh, brother! Would she ever be able to act normally around him again?

As it turned out Rick was fully engaged in keeping control of the boat in the worsening swell so there was no time for conversation, awkward or otherwise. The sky was grey and the wind was brisk, keeping him on his toes. It was far from dangerous but it did require his attention.

She sat up front and worked on her laptop for a bit, but trying to type with the horizon undulating drunkenly played havoc with her equilibrium and wasn't very productive. Even reading through her previous day's work for editing purposes proved impossible to her constitution.

Stella had always possessed an excellent set of sea legs but they'd obviously become rusty from lack of use as nausea sat like a lead sinker in her stomach.

Which at least wiped away the images of Rick showering in the moonlight.

She gave up on the book, shutting her laptop lid.

'Do you want to go down and make sure everything's secured properly below deck?' Rick called out an hour later as she sat very still, keeping her gaze fixed on the horizon, and concentrated on deep breathing.

Stella stood. Good idea. Something to do to keep her mind off the unsettling up and down of the boat.

It started to rain lightly as she passed him and she shivered as the breeze cooled the water droplets on her skin. He'd taken his shirt off at some stage and his chest was speckled with sea spray.

It reminded her of the way water droplets had clung to his naked skin last night and she wondered if they were cool on his skin too. Whether they tasted of salt or of man.

Or some heady mix of both.

If she hadn't felt so rough, she might have been tempted to try. 'Do you want your spray jacket?' she asked, not quite meeting his eyes.

Rick nodded, examining her face. It had gone from pale to white as the sail billowing above their heads. 'Thanks. You okay?' he asked. 'The bureau says it'll only last for another couple of hours.'

Stella gripped the leather back of the high captain's chair

where his butt was parked. He looked totally in his element. Calm and confident. Relishing the inclement weather even, as if it were nothing more than a sun shower. Stella nodded. 'I'm fine.'

He grinned at her, his long hair blowing behind him in true pirate fashion. 'There are some sea sickness pills in the cupboard above the sink,' he offered.

'I'm fine,' she lied.

Rick laughed. 'There's a lot of that going on today.'

Stella was sure if her cheeks weren't so cool they'd be heating up nicely. 'I practically grew up on a boat.'

Rick shrugged. 'Just saying…'

She went below deck and checked every room, securing any items that were lying around. She grabbed her spray jacket and pulled Rick's off the hook on the back of his door and headed to the galley, finding a couple of cans of soup and emptying them into a saucepan. The boat rolled to the side as she placed it over the element and her stomach lurched.

Damn it.

She reached above the sink and threw back two of the little blue pills, praying they'd work in a hurry.

She stood over the soup as it heated, shifting her weight from leg to leg with the motion of the boat. When it was done she puréed it, poured it into thermal mugs, cut off thick chunks of bread from the loaf they'd bought yesterday and loaded it all onto a tray. She shrugged into her jacket and folded his over her arm.

By the time she rejoined him fifteen minutes after taking the anti-emetic she was actually feeling markedly better.

'Thanks,' Rick said, relieving her of the tray and quickly shrugging into the jacket.

She could see water droplets clinging to his eyelashes and spattering his bronzed chest. Just as the shower spray had done last night.

She dragged her eyes away. Must not *think about the shower*.

'Hmm, this is good,' Rick said, watching her face as two pink spots appeared on her pale cheeks. 'I think I'll keep you.'

Stella's gaze flicked to his, to the teasing light in his pirate eyes. Two could play at that game. 'I think I'll let you,' she murmured.

Rick cocked an eyebrow, surprised at her easy comeback, then chuckled. He warmed his hands around the mug, taking another sip of the rich, fragrant pea and ham soup. 'Weather's easing up.'

Stella looked out at the lurching ocean. 'It is?'

He chuckled some more. 'You've become such a landlubber. Can't you feel it beneath your soles?'

Stella felt the laugh reach right inside her and warm her from the inside out. She guessed she had. 'No, Captain Ahab, I can't.'

'Ah, Moby Dick, my favourite book,' he teased, because he knew how much Stella hated it.

She rolled her eyes at him. 'You've never read it.'

'I have,' he protested.

'When?'

'When you dared me to,' he said.

Stella frowned at him, thinking back through the mists of time to that long-ago summer dare. 'I was twelve.'

She'd been going through a classics phase and also trying to read anything nautical to connect with her father, to try and understand why he'd loved the sea more than her mother.

It hadn't helped.

'I never back down on a dare. Besides, I liked it.'

Not as much as the hot pirate sex in Pleasure Hunt...

They had a discussion about its merits while they finished off their lunch and even Stella felt the sea was calmer by the time she reloaded their tray. The wind had definitely dropped. The sprinkling rain had stopped and they shrugged out of their jackets. A bare bicep brushed against her shoulder as he threw his jacket over the back of his chair and she shut her eyes briefly as heat licked at the point of contact.

'I'll get rid of these,' she said briskly, pulling away from him.

Rick watched her go, her hips full and round and swinging enticingly as her gait compensated for the lurch of the boat. Hips that had appeared one summer along with the bra and, no matter how much he'd tried to ignore them in his day-to-day dealings with her, they'd been right there in his fevered teenage dreams.

A sudden gust of wind caused the boat to roll to the side and he watched as she shimmied to counteract the swell. He smiled, admiring the move until he realised she'd overbalanced and was going down.

'Stella!' he called as he sprang from his chair.

Too late. The boat had thrown her sideways and Stella hit the deck hard on her left upper arm, the tray flying as she extended her other hand to buffer the impact, skidding as she grabbed at the wood for purchase.

'Stella,' Rick called again as he threw himself down beside her inert crumpled body, his heart hammering. 'Stella? Are you okay?'

Stella groaned. She couldn't think for the pain in her left arm.

Rick touched her arm, trying to roll her over. 'Stella?'

She moaned and he stopped. 'I'm okay, I'm okay,' she panted. 'Just give me a second.'

'Where are you hurt?' he asked.

'Arm,' she said after a moment. 'Hand.' She looked up at him through her fringe. 'Dignity.'

Rick laughed, relieved that she couldn't be too badly hurt if her sense of humour was still intact. 'Do you think anything's broken?'

Stella zeroed in on the pain in her upper arm where she'd

fallen the hardest. It had initially been excruciating but the intensity had eased quickly. It only felt as if a brick had fallen on it now as opposed to a cement column.

'Let me help you up,' he offered.

Stella acquiesced with a brief nod of her head. With both arms hurting like blazes, she had no idea how she was even going to get up. Rick grabbed her around the waist and gently pulled her into a sitting position. His big warm body was behind hers and for a moment she was so relieved she wasn't destined to spend for ever spread on the deck like a stranded beetle she sagged against him and shut her eyes.

Rick rubbed his cheek against her hair, the scent of coconuts filling his nostrils. He picked up her right hand. The knuckles were grazed and the middle three finger pads were bleeding with splinters embedded in each one.

He tried really hard not to think about Lady Mary and her splinter, but with Stella all warm and pliant against him, smelling like a pina colada, it was hard not to go there.

'Nasty,' he murmured, anticipation already building in his gut, knowing that he was the one who would take them out. Kiss those fingers better just as Vasco had. 'How's your arm? Can you move it?'

Stella gingerly rotated her shoulder. 'Bloody sore,' she bitched.

He smiled into her hair. 'What about your dignity?'

Her arm throbbed and she couldn't even rub it with her opposite hand because it throbbed as well. And was bleeding to boot. 'Unrecoverable, I should imagine.'

He chuckled. 'Nah. You really fell very gracefully.'

'Oh, goody,' she said dryly. 'A critique.'

He laughed again. 'Come on. Let's get you down below and have a look at you.'

'I bet you say that to all the girls,' she muttered.

Stella blinked as the snappy rejoinder loaded with innuendo slipped from her mouth. What the?

He laughed some more. 'Just the ones who fall at my feet.'

Rick helped her up. The boat rolled again slightly and he grabbed her waist and her good arm to steady her as she wobbled against him. He sucked in a breath as, for a moment, every part of her from her soft breasts to her round hips was pressed against him.

He took a step back as his body leapt to life. 'You've got your sea legs?' he asked.

Stella nodded. 'Sorry 'bout that.'

'No worries.' He shrugged. 'Why don't you go on down? I'll fix a few things up here and then I'll join you.'

Stella, despite the throb in her arm and the sting in her fingers, was still stuck back in that moment.

She nodded her head dumbly.

No dignity anywhere in sight!

When Rick joined her half an hour later she'd recovered sufficiently to have taken some painkillers, located the first-aid kit, washed her hand in the sink and was sitting at the table valiantly trying to dig the splinters out. But trying to do it left-handed was a slow enough process without being hampered by a restricted range of movement from the soft tissue damage inflicted by the fall up higher, near her shoulder.

Rick shoved his hands on his hips. 'What are you doing?' he asked.

Stella, who had made more of a mess through pricking herself, was not in the best of moods. It really didn't help that he looked all hot and sexy in that shirtless way of his.

'What do you think?' she demanded. 'I'm trying to get the splinters out.'

Rick smiled down at the petulant set to her mouth. *Oh, goody, this was going to be fun.*

'Here,' he said, scooting her along the bench seat as he moved in beside her. 'Let me.' Rick held out his hand. When she didn't comply he gave her an impatient look. 'Stella?'

Stella was in a quandary as the scene she'd written for *Pleasure Hunt* looked as if it too was about to play out. Well, the G-rated version of it anyway.

She couldn't imagine Rick sucking her fingers into his mouth. Well…she could. And she had. She'd even written it down.

But that was Vasco.

Rick could almost read the thoughts in her very expressive eyes. She was torn between medical necessity and curiosity. 'You don't want them to fester, do you?' he asked innocently.

Stella swallowed as she offered him her palm, hoping that she was submitting purely on medical grounds but knowing there were other less sensible, less pure reasons.

She just prayed he never read her book.

Her palm was warm in his as Rick took an antiseptic swab and cleaned up the site so he had a clearer field of vision. This close, like Vasco, he could see Stella's mouth and the way her teeth dug into her bottom lip.

He raised an eyebrow. 'You ready for this?' he asked.

Stella doubted she'd ever be ready for Rick being this close, his sea-salt-and-ocean-spray aroma wrapping her in a hundred childhood memories that warred with the very adult visions of him naked beneath a shower.

'I promise I'll be gentle,' he murmured.

Stella rolled her eyes at the amused glitter in his tropical gaze. The only way she was going to survive being the sole focus of his stymied flirting reflex was to give as good as she got. 'Maybe I don't like it gentle.'

Rick's heart thunked hard in his chest as he pulled back a little in surprise. She had her eyebrow raised and a small smile playing on her lips.

She was flirting back.

He chuckled. It had been a long time since they'd traded banter like this. It made his plan that much more enticing.

As Vasco had, he ducked his head and leaned over her

hand. Given that his deck was much more polished than that of a pirate ship from the seventeen hundreds, the splinters were much smaller than the one Mary had embedded in her finger. Certainly they were not removable by his teeth and it took some time digging them out.

She didn't whimper or complain although Rick looked up at one stage and she had her eyes shut and face screwed up. Their legs brushed intermittently beneath the table, their upper bodies were almost touching, his head was level with her cleavage and he wondered what she'd do if he claimed that long-awaited kiss early.

Find out if her mouth tasted as sweet as it looked. If it really did taste like coconuts.

Stella opened her eyes and caught him looking at her. Her breath caught in her throat. 'What?' she asked.

Rick took a moment or two to answer. Then he shook his head and said, 'Nothing,' and returned to his ministration, his hand not quite as steady.

Another ten minutes saw the job done. 'There now,' he announced to her closed eyes. 'Isn't that better?'

Stella looked down at her hand, the splinters gone from the pads of her fingers, his thumb lightly brushing her palm— just as Vasco's had done. The instinct to shut her eyes and allow her body to feel the caress everywhere warred with her guilt about indulging another Vasco fantasy with an unsuspecting Rick.

It made her crazy.

And the pain made her bitchy.

'No,' she said testily. 'It bloody hurts, actually.'

Rick felt her trying to withdraw her hand from his but he resisted her attempt, knowing it was too good an opportunity to pass up. 'Fine,' he sighed, 'I'll just have to kiss them better.'

It took a moment for his intention to register and another moment for Stella to open her mouth and lodge a protest. But by then it was too late. He was lifting her fingers to his mouth, holding her gaze as he did so. Her protest stuttered to an inarticulate gurgle as his lips briefly brushed over first one fingertip, then the next. When he got to the third her eyes widened as she felt his tongue press against the pad, laving the wound gently before his lips met then slowly withdrew.

She made some noise at the back of her throat that sounded foreign in the charged atmosphere between them.

It might have been a whimper.

'There,' he said huskily, her dilated pupils not only doing funny things to his groin, but deep inside his chest too. 'Is that better?'

She wanted to shake her head, tell him no. That they burned. That he'd set them on fire. But she was only capable of a nod. A very weak nod.

'Good,' Rick said with difficulty as her mouth hovered so very close and that line became even hazier.

My pleasure.

CHAPTER SEVEN

Lady Mary sat awkwardly on the chair placed in the middle of the sun-drenched deck, conscious of the crew's barely concealed curiosity.

'You'll have to lean back,' Vasco said from behind her.

Mary turned slightly, catching him in her peripheral vision. 'Really, I don't think this is necessary,' she protested primly, her hands folded in her lap.

Vasco placed his hand on her shoulder, urging her back. 'The lady wishes to wash her hair. What the lady wants, the lady gets.'

Mary submitted to the pressure of his hand and turned to face the front again. 'I am perfectly capable of washing my own hair, Captain Ramirez.'

Vasco leaned down, his lips near her ear, inhaling the floral scent of her, so utterly female in this all-male environment. 'Ah, but where would the fun be in that, Mary?'

He smiled at her slight intake of breath at his familiarity. 'Undo your hair,' he ordered in a low whisper. 'Lie back.'

Mary felt her nipples pebble against the fabric of her chemise at the deep vein of risqué in the low command. Another protest rose to her lips but she stifled it. In her week on the ship she'd learned that the Spanish captain always got what he wanted.

And her hair really did need a wash.

Her fingers trembled as she pulled out the pins that secured her hair in an elaborate up do, one by one. She could hear her own breath loud in her ears as he towered above her. When it was all released she shook it out, then furrowed her fingers into the back of the curly mass to loosen any recalcitrant strands.

She became aware that the low chatter from the crew had stopped and she was the object of their blatant attention. 'Captain,' she said, feeling suddenly breathless, 'your men are staring.'

Vasco couldn't blame them. Her hair was like a Titan masterpiece, a flaming torch beneath the blazing sun burnishing the highlights into strands of golden thread.

He gently picked up a long spiral curl from her shoulder and pulled it out to its full length before letting it go, watching it recoil against the scarlet fabric of her frock.

'It's not often they see a woman of such beauty, madam.'

'I would prefer they did not,' she said, reaching for just the right amount of haughty as the low, almost reverent compliment unsettled her.

Vasco preferred they did not as well and he barked some orders at them, more than satisfied with the immediate response.

'Thank you,' Mary murmured as a dozen or so crew got back to their jobs.

'What the lady wants...'

He looked down at her crowning glory and imagined how it would look spread over the milky skin of her breasts. What would she want when he was looking at her like that?

For she would soon be his.

'Tip your head back.'

The command was betrayed by the roughness of his

*voice and he expected her to object yet again. When
she acquiesced without dissent, her hair falling over
the back of the chair in a soft red wave, his anticipation
built another notch. It had been many months since he'd
last had a woman. And never in all his eight and twenty
years had he ever had a creature so stunningly beautiful.*

*He picked up the bucket and poured the water slowly
onto her hair, distributing it evenly, watching as the
curls became drenched and the whole glorious mass
darkened into a lustrous sheath of the finest satin. The
excess pooled around his boots but didn't register as
an errant droplet captured his gaze. It trickled onto
her forehead and began a slow descent down her face,
running over a closed eyelid, down one creamy cheek
until it reached her mouth, where her tongue darted
out, sipping it up.*

*Vasco almost threw the bucket down and lowered his
mouth to claim those moist, upturned lips on the spot.
The desire to kiss her, to ravage that tempting mouth,
had been building for days. But even through the savage haze of lust that had set a raging inferno in his loins
he knew that she wasn't ready. That the dance wasn't
yet complete.*

*So he picked up the soap and rubbed it over the sod-
den silky layers. Then he dropped it into the bucket and
let his hands take over.*

*Mary almost moaned as Vasco's hands furrowed into
her hair, the pads of his fingers rubbing with sensual
ease against her scalp. Her nipples and belly tightened.
Goose flesh broke out everywhere. Quite why she had
no idea, given she was hotter than she'd ever been.*

The sun no doubt.

*Nothing to do with his gaze, which she knew without
having to open her eyes lay heavily on the pulse drum-
ming a frantic tattoo at the base of her neck.*

'How's that?' he murmured.

At some level, Mary knew she should be contained in her reply but the drugging magic of his touch, the aroma of lavender and chives and the warmth of the sun were addling her senses. 'Amazing,' she breathed and Vasco chuckled.

At home this would have been her maid's job, and it would never have felt this...decadent.

And Vasco certainly was nobody's servant.

Her aunt would have an attack of the vapours if she could see the pirate laying his hands on her niece in such a familiar fashion. But Mary, for one, was giving herself up to the experience as she angled her head down to allow him access to where hair met nape.

Vasco's soapy fingers massaged her hairline, dipping down to rub the back of her neck, and he swallowed as a sigh escaped her lips. He noticed how her hands clenched and unclenched the fabric at her lap, the agitated press of her cleavage against the prison of her neckline, and sensed she was feeling things she'd never before experienced.

He worked his way back up to her temples, slowly stroking her there, working his way down to the shell of her ear, drifting his thumb across its ridges, smiling as he heard the rough inward drag of her breath.

He leaned down, replacing his fingers with his lips. 'You are very beautiful, Mary.'

Mary opened her eyes as his words slithered like the serpent into every cell in her body. A dozen retorts came to mind. He should not be talking to her like this. But with his hands creating havoc and her body craving something she didn't understand only one thing came to her lips. She turned her head slightly, their mouths closer than was decent.

'So are you, Vasco, so are you.'
For he was, quite simply, the most beautiful man she'd ever seen.

AFTER two more days of similar weather they finally had a calm, sunny day and Stella was able to get out on deck, where she felt most inspired, to do some more writing.

Which was just as well because she was going totally stir crazy.

She'd spent a lot of time down below during the inclement weather, trying to type two-fingered in between doses of pain-killers as her arm swelled up and the bruising came out. Rick, worried that she'd broken her humerus, had wanted to turn back and get her some medical help but Stella had refused.

Yes, she'd fallen heavily and yes, the pain had increased since the swelling and bruising had come out, but she'd broken her radius a few years ago and her current pain was nothing like how excruciating that had been.

She was sure she hadn't broken it. She'd assured him all she needed was a few days for the swelling to go down and she'd be back to normal.

But in the meantime, even the most basic things had been difficult and she was cranky and out of sorts with her limited abilities. Rick, in true Vasco fashion, had gallantly offered to help her dress and bathe, which she declined not quite in the same spirit it was offered.

So she'd battled on by herself, making do with quick showers and dressing in sarongs that required minimal arm lift. More complicated things like shaving her legs and washing her hair seemed like distant luxuries.

It was most frustrating on the writing front. The words were flowing in her head but she just couldn't get them down quick enough and the grazed knuckles and sore finger pads of her right hand made typing slow and laborious. Every twenty minutes she'd had to stop and let her left hand take over, but it caused the throbbing to increase up higher and after about ten minutes she had to take a break.

So, it felt good indeed to have the sun on her face and the feel of a calm ocean beneath her feet again and for the first half hour they got under way she just sat in her low chair with her face turned to the sun, soaking it up.

But it was all downhill from the moment she opened her laptop. It didn't take long for her mood to evaporate as her useless fingers, despite the absolutely exhilarating day, made a hard slog of the writing process. And when her arm started to throb half an hour into the process she shut the lid of the laptop in disgust.

It had felt really good this morning too. The bruising was fading to a greeny-yellow and the swelling had reduced by about half. She could even lift her bent arm almost level with her shoulder before discomfort forced her to stop.

'You okay?'

She turned to see Rick coming up behind her, taking full advantage of the glorious weather by once again going shirtless. She winced as the sudden movement wrenched through her arm. 'Fine,' she said morosely as she blew her fringe out of her eyes on a huffed breath.

Even it was annoying her. It was strawy and scratchy from the rigors of sea salt and the tangling effect of ocean breezes. Conscious of needing to save water on a boat, she hadn't washed it since they'd left Cairns.

Rick chuckled as he sat beside her. 'You don't seem fine.' He laughed again at her responding scowl. 'Come on, what's up? Tell Uncle Rick.'

'The words are coming but my useless fingers can't type them fast enough.'

'I could type them,' he offered. 'You can dictate them to me.' He smiled at her. 'It'll be just like Barbara Cartland.'

Stella rolled her eyes. No way in the world was she ever going to let him anywhere near Lucinda and Inigo.

Rick grinned. 'I'll take that as a no, then. What else?'

'My arm hurts,' she said, aware that it could be interpreted as whining. 'And my head is as itchy as hell because it hasn't been washed in for ever and I can't even scratch it because my fingers are too sore.'

For a moment Rick couldn't believe his luck. He'd read the scene where Vasco washed Lady Mary's hair about a dozen times. He let his gaze run idly over her hair, chunks of it escaping a poorly placed plastic claw. 'Well, now, that *is* something I can help with,' he said, very matter-of-fact.

She glared at him. 'Offering to help me shower was not funny the first time,' Stella said grouchily.

'Oh, I don't know.' Rick shrugged. 'I kind of thought it was but,' he said, holding up his hand to still the protest about to come out of her mouth, 'I didn't mean that. I'll wash it up here, on deck.' He grinned at her. 'You'll be fully clothed, I promise.'

Stella stilled as the implications of his offer slowly sank in. Another Vasco and Mary moment. She searched his tropical blue gaze for a spark of recognition. Something that told her he knew what he was offering was far from innocent. He looked back at her with the same clear, blue-eyed brilliance as always.

She chewed on her lip as the idea teased at her conscience. 'What…you mean with a…bucket?' she asked.

Rick bit the inside of his cheek as he struggled to stay deadpan for her searching gaze. He returned her interest with his best I-have-no-idea-what-you're-talking-about look. 'No…' He pointed to the stern on the boat. 'With the shower.'

She turned gingerly this time to take in the metallic head under which she'd watched him shower the other night. Her cheeks heated as the illicit image revisited.

Rick decided to leap on her indecision and take charge, giving her no quarter. The boat was on autopilot and it was clear sailing today. 'You head on over, I'll get your shampoo. It's in your en suite, yes?'

Stella nodded dumbly, sitting in her chair unmoving, as Rick disappeared. Could she indulge herself for a third time? This voyage was turning into some kind of hedonistic exploration of her fantasies.

It was…immoral, surely?

Debauched, certainly.

Rick came back on deck and smiled to see her still sitting in the same spot, indecision on her face. 'Come on,' he called. 'I don't have all day.'

Stella turned to look at his naked back as he headed towards the stern. She stood automatically to his command, dragging her chair with her. He looked so much like Vasco when she reached him, her conscience piqued.

'I don't think this is a good idea.'

Rick doubted he'd ever heard a more feeble protest and knew he was going to have to hold her hand on this one.

'Are you crazy? It's a brilliant idea. The sun is out, there's a light breeze, it'll dry quickly. And as there's nothing I can do about your arm or help with your writing, you should let me do this.'

Plus, you want to.

He took the chair out of her unprotesting fingers and placed it under the shower head, busying himself with finding the right position. By the time he was done she seemed to have resigned herself to a little piece of *Pleasure Hunt*. She sat when he asked her and even snuggled down low in her chair so just her neck and shoulders were exposed above the canvas and her head could tilt back easily over the edge.

Of course that bent her sarong-clad body into a banana shape with her feet flat on the deck, her thighs bent before him like an offering from the gods. Thighs that her sarong fell away from, leaving them exposed to his view. Not skinny. Firm, rounded like her and smooth with the beginnings of a tan tinting the formerly milky skin.

He turned the water on and doused himself with it first before removing the hand-held head from its cradle, kneeling behind her and directing the spray at her hair. She startled slightly and he swallowed as he noticed her nipples pucker beneath the sarong. 'Too cold?'

Stella reined in her heartbeat as his hand sifted through her hair, wishing she could rein in her other bodily responses as easily. 'No. Just wasn't expecting it.'

'Sorry,' he said, his gaze fixed on the two round points tenting the fabric at her chest. 'Should have warned you.'

Should have warned myself.

He might have been doing this as a tease but he hadn't been immune to that hair-washing scene and already he could feel a tightening in his groin.

Stella shut her eyes tight as his hand sifted and lifted and caressed every strand of her hair to ensure it was waterlogged. His fingers occasionally brushed against her scalp and she squeezed her thighs together as the sensation seemed to travel straight to a point between her legs.

Like acupuncture. Or reflexology.

Whatever…he'd definitely found her sweet spot.

Rick flicked the taps off, determinedly dragging his gaze away from her thighs and nipples and fixing it on her hair, on the job at hand, determined not to get carried away by it.

She was supposed to be turned into a panting mess—not him.

'Shampoo now,' he said as he squirted a healthy dollop into his palm and a waft of coconut—of her—hit him square in the solar plexus. It was like liquid silk in his hands and he spread it over her sodden hair evenly before he started to rub it into a lather with the flat of his palms.

Stella almost sighed at his touch. His movements were brisk at first, but after a few moments they changed, became slower, more defined, the tips of his fingers dragging with languorous subtlety against her scalp. She felt the motion right down to her toes and all the hot spots in between.

Every cell went on high alert. Her back arched involuntarily as she bit back a whimper. The pain in her arm and the sting in her fingers floated away on a sexual high.

Shampoo foamed between Rick's fingers as he watched her shift restlessly in the chair. The image of him sliding his soapy hands onto her shoulders, over her chest, pushing the sarong down off her breasts and lathering them up, teasing the nipples into taut peaks until she orgasmed hit him out of the blue and the tightness became something more.

He was harder than the wood beneath his knees.

He needed to distract himself fast. 'You always had gorgeous hair,' he murmured as the thickness of it filled his palms. He remembered diving with her when they'd been kids and being mesmerised by the way her hair streamed behind her as she swam or floated around her like a crown when she stopped. He'd dreamt of it often during his teenage years. 'Just like that mermaid you always wanted to be.'

Good. That was good.

Reminding himself of why it would be a very bad idea to lean over as Vasco had also wanted to do and ravage her mouth.

Because they were friends. Long-term friends.

He was just having some fun.

Stella opened her eyes, thinking back to those days when she'd truly believed in the imaginary world they'd created. Instead of having to create this faux fantasy life to keep that connection alive.

'Everything was so simple back then,' she murmured.

Rick nodded. Back then he'd been plain Rick, she'd been Nathan's daughter and hadn't had breasts and hips. Now he was Vasco Ramirez, Nathan was dead and she had breasts, hips and a lot of other bits in between.

She bent her head forward, just as Lady Mary had done and he obliged, caressing her hairline, drifting his thumbs over her nape, going lower, kneading his fingers into the muscles of her neck and lower still to her shoulders.

'Mmm,' she groaned. 'That feels good.'

She couldn't help herself, it just tumbled out. Because it did feel good, it felt so damn good *everywhere* she wanted to turn around and French him as she almost had all those years ago, and decades of being buddies and business partners and all those other consequences be damned.

Rick swallowed. 'That's because you're so tense,' he said lightly, feeling pretty damn tense himself but working on the knots in her neck muscles until he had them all ironed out because she kept making these little gurgly noises at the back of her throat that he could really become addicted to.

By the time they were gone and he'd forced himself to turn on the spray he had an erection that could have been used on Vasco's pirate ship as the plank for prisoners to walk to their doom upon.

For his own sanity, he tried to make the conditioning process much faster but pretty much failed. She had her hands stuffed between her thighs and he spent the whole time wondering if she really was just holding her sarong in place or maybe easing a little ache down there.

His imaginings had gone from lathering her breasts to his head disappearing between those amazing thighs and he was fit to burst when he left her, hair brushed and drying off, in the sunshine.

'Thank you,' she called after his disappearing back.

Rick gave her a wave, not turning around because he looked perfectly indecent at the moment and probably would be for quite a while with her squirmy, back-archy thing imprinted on his retinas. 'My pleasure,' he murmured quietly to himself as he descended below deck as quickly as his legs would carry him.

* * *

At midnight Rick gave up trying to sleep and trudged up to the deck to lie under the stars for a while. They'd always had a calming effect and he needed that badly at the moment, when his body was raging with undiluted lust and no amount of diversion tactics seemed to be working.

The ocean was still and the night almost silent as he made his way to the middle of the deck. He could barely feel the bob of the boat beneath his back and his breath was loud in his head. The waning moon threw a narrow beam of light on the surface of the gently rippling water as it fought for space in the crowded sky.

He lay with his knees bent and took a deep steadying breath.

Now, *this* made sense.

Stella and what happened to him every time he looked at her didn't make sense at all.

But this—the ocean—did.

This was like coming home.

He remembered turning up at Dartmouth at the age of fifteen, a rucksack on his back and four pounds in his pocket. He'd hitched from London the previous day. Nathan had looked at him from the deck of the *Persephone* and said, 'Sophia's been on the phone to me.'

He'd looked at Nathan with mutiny in his eyes. He'd loved his grandmother, but she hadn't understood that the ocean ran in his veins. She'd wanted him to study hard and go to university and all he'd wanted was a sea breeze in his hair. He'd chafed against her bonds. Cut classes. Flunked out.

'I'm not going back. This is where I belong.'

Nathan had looked at him for long moments. 'It's not the glamorous life it seems on summer break or from your father's grandiose sea stories, Rick. You should be in school.'

He'd shaken his head. He'd always known from Nathan's quiet restraint that his father's embellishments were romantic sentimentality and that there wasn't a lot of romance or sentiment in salvaging. He'd learned early it was ninety-nine per cent grunt, one per cent glory. 'I should be here. The business is half mine.'

They'd both known that Rick didn't legally inherit until he was of age but Nathan hadn't called him on it.

'That it is. But are you man enough?'

Rick had nodded his head firmly. 'Yes, sir.'

Nathan had crossed his arms. 'You come on board, you answer to me.'

'Aye, aye, captain.'

'And you finish school.' Nathan had raised his hand at the objections that had been about to tumble from Rick's mouth. 'A man knows the importance of education, Rick.' He'd shoved a hand on his hip and said, 'Take it or leave it.'

Rick had bristled at the harshness of it when he'd reluctantly agreed and had done his lessons by correspondence with less than good grace, but he'd been grateful for the many years that Nathan had forced his hand.

It hadn't been until years later that he'd found out Nathan and Sophia had done a deal while he'd been hitching his way to Dartmouth. Nathan had promised to look after Rick and see that he finished school and Sophia had agreed to loosen the reins she'd held on her stubborn grandson.

Nathan had had the utmost respect for Rick's Spanish grandmother, who had selflessly taken care of him when her daughter, Carmela's, tempestuous love affair with Anthony Granville had finished and neither had known what to do with a toddler. Rick knew now that if Sophia had demanded that Nathan bring her grandson back then he would have been back in London faster than he'd been able to blink.

Nathan had always said to never get between a woman and her child but he had still gone into bat for Rick. Had been the father his own father had never been. Had been his family after Sophia had passed away the following year.

So, messing around with Nathan's daughter was not the way he repaid the man, even if it was just a bit of teasing.

That was getting out of hand.

Remembering what made sense—the pulse of the ocean, the business, Inigo's treasure—that was how he repaid him.

It was just a little difficult at the moment with so little to do on a boat that virtually sailed itself and a barely dressed first mate who didn't seem like so much of a mate any more. In a few days they'd be at their destination in Micronesia and then he'd have things to do other than look at Stella all day in hardly any clothes.

They'd both be occupied. Their days filled with diving and poring over charts and Nathan's research trying to pinpoint *The Mermaid*.

In the meantime he really needed to stop reading *Pleasure Hunt*.

Stella kicked at the sheets restlessly, straining to hear any more movement from above deck. She'd heard Rick's footsteps twenty minutes ago after hours of staring at the ceiling, trying not to think about how his hands had felt on her scalp. How if she just shut her eyes she could be Mary and he could be Vasco and how maybe they could skip a few chapters and she could be tied to his bed.

She shut her eyes and erased the image. She was taking shameful advantage of the situation. Indulging her fantasies when Rick was just being himself. The guy she'd always known. A friend. One who would do anything for her. From coming to tell her personally about her father's sudden death to washing her hair because it was scratchy and itchy and she was physically limited.

Still, there was a part of her, egged on by her hormones and a latent wicked streak, that couldn't help but speculate. Just what would he do? How far would he go? Would he cut up those ripe mangoes that they'd purchased in Moresby and that permeated the galley with sweet promise and feed them to her as Vasco had done with a juicy pear? Would he scratch that itch that drove her mad right in the centre of her back that she just couldn't reach with her current injuries?

And what about that other itch that seemed to build and build the longer she spent in his company? The one that tingled between her thighs, that made her breasts feel heavy, that caused an ache down deep and low somewhere behind her belly button?

Would he relieve that if she asked him?

Because she wasn't even capable of that at the moment and God knew she was fit to burst.

Not that helping herself was ever as good as the real thing. But it was better than death by deprivation.

Damn it!

She kicked the sheets off. This was insane. Lying here thinking about Rick like this was pure madness. Neither of them was ever going to do anything that ruined twenty-plus years of friendship so she just needed to get over herself.

She needed to go on deck and normalise their relationship. Lying in her bed, her body throbbing, put images in her head that didn't have any place in reality. Lying on deck, looking at the stars with him as she'd done a hundred times before, would help to put things into perspective.

And God knew, if her body couldn't have passion then it sure as hell needed perspective.

Rick heard the bell before she made it to the top of the stairs. He shut his eyes and prayed to Neptune for restraint.

'Hey,' he said as she tramped over, eyes staring doggedly at the sky.

'Hey,' Stella acknowledged as she drew level and looked down at him. 'Can't sleep?'

'Something like that,' he said as her face appeared in his line of vision. She was wearing some three-quarter-length grey pants, the fabric of which was quite thin, clingy around the thighs, loose around the calves. And what he could only describe as a boob tube.

'Neither can I. Want some company?'

'Sure.'

He was already burning in the fires of hell—what was one more lie?

Stella joined him on her back on the deck, making sure her injured left arm was on the outer and that she maintained some distance between them. Rick and her didn't really do distance so it seemed awkward.

'Any shooters tonight?'

He nodded. 'Saw one earlier.'

'Did you make a wish?' she asked, rolling her head towards him.

Not one that he could repeat in decent company. He turned his head too. 'I wished for—'

'Stop,' Stella said urgently, automatically silencing him with the press of a finger against his lips. A finger that still stung a little and protested the movement. 'You know you're not supposed to say.'

Rick stilled as her fingerprint seared into the DNA of his lips. There were a lot of things he wasn't supposed to say.

Or do.

And every single one of them begged to be ignored.

Stella's eyes widened as a glitter of something distinctly sexual enriched his blue gaze with something distinctly pirate.

Heat flared in her belly and breasts.

Between her legs.

And deep, deep inside.

So deep she doubted anyone had ever touched it.

Her gaze narrowed to his mouth as her finger moved of its own volition, tracing his lips, the sting instantly easing. She could feel the warmth of his breath against it, the roughness of every inhalation and exhalation.

Rick opened his mouth slightly, giving silent permission to that seeking finger. When it had circumnavigated every millimetre he grazed the tip gently with his teeth as he touched his tongue to where the splinter had been.

The way she stared at his mouth as if it were the most perfect creation went straight to his head. The sound of her indrawn breath travelled straight to his groin.

He swallowed as a jungle drum beat in his head and thudded through his chest. 'Stella.'

'Hmm?' she asked absently as she mapped his mouth with her gaze. Vasco's mouth.

Rick tried again. 'I don't think we should—'

This time she didn't cut him off with her finger. This time she used her mouth and Rick was totally unprepared. He'd always dreamt their mythical first kiss would be soft and gentle. Tentative. It was certainly the way he would have kissed her at sixteen. But there was nothing tentative about the way she opened up to him.

In seconds the kiss was wet and deep and hard, leaving no room for finesse or wishing on stars. There was just feeling, reacting. Letting all that suppressed desire bubble up on a wave of coconut and take him to a higher plane.

Stella moaned as fantasy fused into reality on a rush of high octane lust that blasted heat into every cell of her body.

And it was better than she'd ever imagined.

The dare faded as they both collected on the prize early.

Desire coursed through her bloodstream and she gasped against his mouth as Rick rolled up onto his elbow, his face looming over hers, his fingers furrowing into her hair.

She sucked in great slabs of air as the kiss robbed her of breath. They both did. Their breathing loud as they rode the dizzying heat and the high oxygen demand of the incendiary kiss. His lips were demanding against hers and she opened to him wider, revelling in the thrust and tangle of his tongue, her head lifting off the deck trying to match it.

Trying to lead. Trying to follow.

Trying to get closer.

She squeezed her thighs together as the heat there morphed into a tingling that became more unbearable with every second. Her pelvic floor muscles undulated with each swipe of his tongue and she pressed her hips firmly into the deck to soothe the pressure building deep and low.

Was it possible to orgasm from a kiss alone?

God knew she'd fantasised about his kiss often enough both as a teenager and as a writer crafting all those highly sensual, gloriously descriptive love scenes. Maybe it was?

His thumb stroked along her temple and her head spun from the rhythmic caress. Her hips rotated restlessly against the deck as she felt herself edge closer.

Maybe, after all this time, a kiss *was* going to be enough?

Rick had spent a good portion of his life *not* wondering what kissing Stella would be like and now he knew he *never* wanted to stop.

Suddenly it was the *only* thing that made sense. Not the stars or the ocean or Inigo's treasure.

None of it.

Just that little whimpering noise at the back of her throat that reverberated inside his head like a benediction—like his own private cheer squad.

And the sweet aroma of coconuts.

Lying by himself on deck before, Stella hadn't made sense.

Looming over her, pressing her into the deck, feeling the flesh and blood of her, the restless sexuality bubbling in her kiss, the harsh, desperate suck of her breath and the answering rhythm of his own body, she'd never made more sense.

He wanted more. He wanted all. He wanted everything.

His hand fell to her arm, to gather her closer, pull her nearer, imprint her along the length of him.

And then she stiffened against him, cried out, broke away…

CHAPTER EIGHT

Rɪᴄᴋ froze as he stared down at her, her right hand supporting her injured left arm, her teeth sunken into her bottom lip, plump and moist from his ravaging. He was dazed for a moment, trying to compute what had brought an abrupt end to the passion.

Trying to compute what the hell had happened in the first place.

'I'm fine,' Stella said, breathing hard through clenched teeth as the jarring settled. She could see his bewilderment and something else, a slow dawning that seemed to closely resemble horror.

No, no, no.

'Just give me a moment,' she scrambled to assure him as she watched his blue gaze lose its drugged lustre and slowly recoil from her. 'Now.' She smiled up at him, the pain in her left arm easing as she slipped her good hand onto his shoulder. 'Where were we?'

Rick shook his head to clear the remnants of a very powerful buzz. *What the hell?* He groaned as he collapsed back against the deck.

'Oh, my God,' he said to the sky, blind to the beauty of the celestial display.

'Rick,' she assured him again, brushing a finger against his hand, 'it's fine.'

'Oh, my God,' he repeated, moving his hand to his face,

covering his eyes and shaking his head from side to side. 'What have I done?'

'Rick—'

'No.' He vaulted upright, then sprang to his feet. 'No, Stella,' he said, looking down at her. 'This is…crazy.'

Stella blinked at his vehemence. It had been shocking and surprising and unexpected. Not to mention unbelievably good. *But crazy?*

She sat up gingerly. Obviously this wasn't going any further and she couldn't have this conversation with him towering over her reclined body.

'Why?'

Rick stared at her as her calm response filled him with complicated angst. 'Because,' he spluttered, 'you're Stella and I'm Rick and *we*—' he pointed back and forth between the two of them '—don't do this.'

'We made a kiss a stake in your flirting dare,' she pointed out.

And as far as Stella was concerned it was the best first kiss ever. A kiss that had obliterated Dale's best for eternity. A kiss that would surely ruin her for all other kisses.

Rick shook his head vehemently. 'Not this kind of kiss.' He'd thought about how it might go down and it hadn't been anything like this. It had been slow, sweet, controlled.

And they'd both been vertical.

'Why not?' She wasn't sixteen any more. Did he think she'd be satisfied with something chaste?

He blanched at her simple query. 'How about twenty-plus years of friendship? Or a legal document with both our signatures on that states we own a company together? Your father, for crying out loud.'

Stella frowned. 'My father?'

'Yes,' Rick fumed.

'My father?'

Rick nodded. 'He warned me off.'

'My *father* warned you off?'

Rick hadn't been forthcoming about what Nathan had said to him that day and, with the slight impression that she too had somehow let her father down, she hadn't pursued it.

He glared at her incredulous expression. 'Well, not in so many words, no. But every crew member he employed knew you were off-limits, Stel. Nathan didn't want anyone messing with his little girl.'

It took her a moment to process that. Would Rick have made a move a long time ago had her father not been all Neanderthal about his daughter?

She'd known there was an undercurrent between them as teenagers but it had all ended abruptly that day and she'd figured it was for the best.

But maybe Rick had always pondered the what-ifs too?

Stella used her right hand to push up from the deck, wincing slightly. 'Well, I don't know if you've noticed, but I'm not a little girl any more, Rick. And my father is dead.'

Rick's gaze dropped involuntarily to her boob tube. 'Yeah.' He grimaced as he returned his gaze to her face. 'I noticed.'

Stella laughed at his forlorn reply. 'I got breasts, sorry.'

He looked at them again. 'Yes, you did. It was simpler when you didn't.'

She frowned. 'I've had them for a long time, Rick—what changed this time?'

He looked at her. That damn book. *Pleasure Hunt.* Thanks to Nathan and years of platonic childhood memories he'd managed to keep perspective in his dealings with Stella.

Until the book.

But his perspective was currently shot to hell.

'The moonlight?' he lied. He somehow didn't think she'd approve of him using her book for his own ends. 'I don't know.' He shrugged. 'I guess it's never been an issue before. We've never been alone before. Not like this.'

She thought about it. 'You're right, I don't think we have.'

They looked at each other for a long moment. 'I think we'd regret it, Stel. In the long run. We have all these great memories of growing up together. Summer holidays on the *Persephone*. Bringing up Spanish coins from the ocean floor. Playing mermaid and pirate.'

Although perhaps that wasn't the best memory to bring up now…

'And when I look at you, that's what I see—how you and your father embraced me as part of the family. They are such fond memories, Stel. They mean a lot to me. I don't want to ruin them by giving in to this…crazy thing. It wouldn't be the same between us any more no matter how hard we tried. And I like what we have.'

Stella knew he was making sense but, right now, she liked what they'd been having five minutes ago more. She could still feel the surge of blood tingle through her breasts and between her thighs. Just the bob of the boat was almost enough to push piano-wire-taut muscles into delicious rapture.

God, why was he so bloody gallant? She'd probably only needed another minute or so and she would have been well satisfied. *Embarrassed for sure*. But not going off to bed with her hormones still raging and bitching at her to boot.

Well, if she had to sit on her hands the next few weeks and pretend that he hadn't almost made her come with just a kiss, then she was damned if she was going to play fair.

'Fine,' she huffed, pushing past him, heading for her cabin. 'Glad I packed my vibrator after all.'

Rick blinked. 'You brought a vibrator?' Hell, she *owned* a vibrator?

She stopped and turned. 'I'm a grown woman, Rick. *I have needs*.' She turned and continued on her way.

Rick shut his eyes on a silent groan as a particularly graphic image entered his head. 'Not helping, Stel,' he called after her, his gaze transfixed by the swing of her hips.

She smiled over her shoulder at him. 'Sweet dreams.'

* * *

Rick did not have a good night.

Every time Stella's bell jingled he strained to hear. What, he wasn't sure. A sigh? A moan? Those soft whimpery noises she made at the back of her throat?

Oh, God, those soft whimpery noises were not conducive to sleep.

And what if he *had* heard them? Would it make it any easier lying alone on the moral high ground knowing she was getting off? Knowing that he could have been in there with her, helping out?

Kissing her more.

Touching her more.

No!

It was hard now but at the end of the voyage and for the rest of the years to come, they'd be glad they were sensible. Glad they hadn't gone past the point of no return.

Maybe one day they'd even laugh about it.

Maybe.

Rick got the boat under way by eight the next morning. Stella hadn't put in an appearance and sitting around thinking about all the reasons she might be sleeping late, including a bone-deep sexual satisfaction, was not improving his mood.

It was another glorious day and losing himself in the familiar routine of setting sail seemed like a better alternative than wondering what mischief Nathan's daughter had got up to between the sheets last night.

And it worked to a degree. Until Stella came on deck an hour later.

In a micro bikini.

He stared at her open-mouthed, pleased for the camouflage of his sunglasses. Two tiny triangles barely contained the swell of her breasts and the pants, high on her leg and low on her front, had two tempting little bows at the side keeping them from falling off altogether.

'Morning,' she said airily as she drew level with him, her laptop, some coconut sunscreen and a towel in hand. A smile on her face. 'What a magnificent day,' she murmured, inhaling the sea air deep into her lungs, feeling it resonate with her spirit.

Rick watched as her chest expanded, straining the fabric of her bikini top to indecent proportions. Lord, *was she trying to give him a heart attack?*

'Sleep well?' he asked, his neutral tone almost killing him.

Stella sighed as the air rushed out of her lungs. 'Like a baby,' she purred.

She hadn't, of course. How could she sleep with a fire ravaging every erogenous zone she owned and quite a few she hadn't even known existed?

She'd barely slept a wink.

Perhaps she should have helped herself as she'd led Rick to believe but, after their near miss, she'd wanted strong male arms and a warm solid chest, not just her and Mr Buzzy.

'How's your arm?' he asked politely.

'Good.' She nodded. It was the first morning it hadn't ached when she woke and the bruising was nearly all faded. She could even move it the full range, if a little gingerly. 'I reckon I can hit my word count today.'

'Better get started, then,' he prompted, desperate to get her coconut aroma and bare shoulder out of his direct line of vision.

Stella nodded, knowing it was best to get away from him yet strangely reluctant to do so. It was as if some tropical fever had her in its grip and he was both the cause and the antidote.

'I might catch some rays first, before the sun gets too hot.'

Of course. Why didn't she just roll around in some jelly while she was at it?

'Yell if you need a hand,' she murmured as she pushed past him, heading for the bow.

He watched her sexy sashay from behind his glasses. *Yell if you need a hand.*

* * *

Stella sun-baked for the first two hours. She wasn't entirely sure what she was playing at but it seemed to have something to do with goading a reaction out of Rick. After all, if he was really that into her, he surely wouldn't be able to ignore her best attempts at extreme flirting?

She shifted, she wiggled, she lay on her back, she rolled over, she sat up, she applied liberal amounts of sunscreen, she even retied the bows.

She got nothing.

Last night had obviously been some sort of anomaly for Rick. A mad moment when a balmy night and the moonshine had affected his judgement. This morning he seemed completely indifferent to her. Nothing like the man who had kissed her as if it were his last day on earth.

Nothing like the guy she'd known for ever either—quick to laugh and eager to share his joy of the ocean. He looked like a robot at the wheel, sunglasses on, scanning the horizon for who knew what. The meaning of life? They'd passed several islands in the distance and they'd slipped by without so much as a *land ahoy* and a finger point.

It was already weird between them and nothing had happened.

Well…nothing much anyway.

She gave up trying eventually and drifted off to sleep, exhausted after her long night of tossing and turning. But later she knew she was going to have to make amends. Get things back on track.

Because, one way or another, she needed him in her life. And if that meant going to her grave without carnal knowledge of one Riccardo Granville, then so be it.

After a day of watching Stella prance around in a bikini, it was a relief to finally drop anchor and go below deck. He had a shower. A very cold shower. And lectured himself on the same things he'd lectured himself about all last night.

This was *Stella*. Nathan's daughter. His old, old friend and business partner.

And no one had ever died from sexual frustration.

By the time he got out of the shower he'd almost convinced himself, then his gaze fell on *Pleasure Hunt* and he was lost again. He picked it up to where it was open. The scene where Vasco fed Lady Mary slices of ripe pear jumped out at him. The scene had been rich with visualisation and Rick had almost been able to smell the sweet pear juice that had trekked down Mary's chin and Vasco had lapped up with his kisses.

Rick shut it for his own sanity. He let his fingers linger over the raised gold lettering of her name. How could he reconcile the Stella Mills who'd written the sexy historical with the Stella Mills he'd known practically all of his life?

How could he ever think of her as sweet and innocent again when he'd been privy to her erotic prose?

When he'd been the subject of that erotic prose?

When the taste of her mouth was imprinted onto his?

He meant what he'd said last night. But he'd never thought it would be so hard. He'd never been obsessed by a woman before. Sure, he'd had his usual teenage infatuations and spent some exciting shore leave with some very generous women, but none had played on his mind like this. None had moved into his brain and taken over.

Stella was fast becoming an obsession.

The question was would the obsession end when they went their separate ways? Or was he destined to wonder for ever?

He shoved the book under his pillow.

Out of sight, out of mind.

Although if he had any sense he'd take it above deck and hurl it into the ocean. But it was Diana's so he couldn't.

At least that was what he told himself anyway.

Stella was throwing a line in over the side when Rick reappeared half an hour later. He looked sublimely sexy in his shirt, regulation boardies and bare feet. God knew why—it wasn't as if he were wearing Armani or Ralph Lauren. But there was something about the way he wore them that oozed a special mix of charisma and wonderful outdoorsy sexuality.

'Thought we'd have some fish tonight,' she said.

Rick nodded. She'd put a button-up throw on over her bikini a long time ago but it was as if he had X-ray vision suddenly and it was still *all* he could see. 'I'll set up the grill.'

An hour later the sky was just starting to blush a velvety pink as they sat on deck and ate their fish with the potatoes that Rick had also fried on the grill. A gentle breeze caressed Stella's neck, lifting the tendrils that had escaped her messily constructed bun. The ocean lapped gently at the hull.

'Did you get your word count done?' Rick asked after they'd been eating in silent contemplation for most of the meal.

Stella nodded, grateful for the conversation. She was excruciatingly aware that they'd been avoiding any mention of what happened last night, which seemed kind of ridiculous sitting together and sharing a meal. 'Just over three thousand words today.'

He took a deep swallow of his beer. 'Is that your usual quota?'

She nodded again. 'I try to do three k a day. Some days—' she grimaced '—that's easier to achieve than others.'

'Why's that?' he asked. 'Surely you just sit there until you reach your goal.'

Stella shook her head at him—such a boy. 'Well, it doesn't really work that way unfortunately.'

He gave her a blank look and she knew she was going to have to explain it to this goal-orientated male.

'It's like diving for lost treasure. Sometimes coins are just lying on the ocean floor ready to scoop up, other times they're locked in chests, which are trapped in impossible-to-reach pockets within an aged, treacherous, waterlogged wreck. They're there…you can see them…but they're tantalisingly out of reach. The muse is like that. Some days she comes out to play and the words flow and other days…' She shrugged. 'It feels like every word is locked away in a chest just out of my reach.'

Rick wondered how quickly some of the *Pleasure Hunt* scenes flowed before stopping himself. 'I don't know,' he joked to cover the errant thoughts. 'You arty types.'

Stella laughed. 'Sorry, I suppose that did sound a bit pretentious.'

From her it had sounded just right. 'Not at all,' he dismissed with a smile. 'Do some scenes flow better than others?' The question slipped out unfiltered and couldn't be recalled.

Stella looked away. The sex scenes in *Pleasure Hunt* had flowed like a gushing tap. Years of feverish fantasies let loose had informed the scenes to embarrassing accuracy. She looked away from the piercing intensity of his gaze.

'No, not really,' she lied, standing to clear the plates. 'They can all be as easy or as difficult as each other.' She balanced the plates a little awkwardly, mindful of her injury and thankful for the calm ocean.

'Here, let me take them,' Rick said as he stood.

She shook her head. 'No way, you cooked, plus you've been waiting on me for days. The arm's heaps better so just sit.' Rick sat and she smiled. 'You want another beer?'

He nodded. 'Sure, why not?' Maybe if he was a little cut he'd go straight to sleep.

Stella seemed to take a while. He could hear her banging around down below deck as the sun gradually set above, the evening sky slowly speckling with stars. It felt oddly domesticated and a deep spring of contentment welled inside him, bringing him to his feet.

He frowned as he prowled restlessly around the deck. The boards felt good beneath his bare feet.

His deck, his boat, his ocean.

These were the things that brought him contentment. Not some woman clattering around in his kitchen.

That never made him feel content.

In fact it usually made him want to get away fast. Ditch the chick at the nearest port and sail himself far away. Get back to his true mistress—the ocean.

Like Nathan. Like his father.

But here he was, nonetheless, on the ocean, sharing it with probably the only woman who truly understood the pull of such a demanding mistress.

The tinkle of her bell alerted him to her presence and he turned to see her walking towards him, holding the necks of two beers in one hand and a plate holding two mangoes, a knife and a cloth in the other.

'I'm having a mango,' she said. 'I wasn't sure if you wanted one or not.' She handed him his beer as she sat on the deck, facing the horizon lotus-style, balancing the plate on her crossed knees.

Rick nodded, taking one as he sat beside her. Not too close. 'Sure, thanks. I'll eat mine after the beer.'

Stella raised the large pungent fruit to her face. It was warm against her cheek and she inhaled deeply. It smelled sweet and wild like forbidden berries and exotic like balmy tropical islands.

'Mmm, that smells good,' she murmured. 'The whole galley smells of them suddenly.'

Rick nodded. He'd noticed earlier when he'd gone below but he didn't want to look at her getting all breathy and orgasmic over anything other than him, so he hung his head back and kept his eyes firmly trained on the sky.

Stella placed the mango on the plate, salivating at the thought of the sweet, warm fruit sliding against her palate. She cut into the soft flesh, a pearl of juice beaded around the incision as the strong aroma wafted out to envelop her in its heady fragrance.

She was conscious of Rick beside her not saying anything. Conscious of what happened between them last night when they'd been on this deck. Conscious that it had sat large between them all day, screwing with their usual effortless dynamic. Normally by now Rick would be talking about the stars or prattling on about Inigo and *The Mermaid*.

Instead they sat in silence as they had done for most of their meal.

Stella took a deep breath as she picked up one mango cheek and scored the flesh. They couldn't go on like this. 'About last night…'

Rick's breath seized in his lungs momentarily and he took a moment before looking at her, taking a swallow of beer to calm himself. 'What about last night?'

Stella didn't dare look at him. The weight of his gaze was intimidating enough. 'You were right,' she said, scoring the other cheek. 'We would regret crossing the line. I'm sorry I made it difficult for you.'

Rick swallowed as she picked up a scored mango cheek, inverted it and used her tongue and teeth to liberate a cube of the soft pungent flesh. 'Yes,' he said faintly, trying not to think of the pear scene in *Pleasure Hunt* he'd not long been skimming.

Stella would have sighed as the fruit zinged along her taste-buds if the topic of conversation weren't so damn serious. She turned to face him as she sucked another cube of mango into her mouth and savoured it. 'I mean, of course it would be awkward between us and would negate all the good memories we've ever made.'

She bit into another perfectly square piece of mango flesh.

Rick heard the soft squelch go right to his groin. He zeroed in on her mouth, which glistened with ripe juice. His fingers tightened around the beer bottle. 'Uh-huh,' he said, not really even listening, his reasoning dissolving into a red haze as her mouth and tongue slowly devoured the fruit.

Vasco had fed Lady Mary, taunting her with slithers of pear, inching them closer, stroking them against her moist lips, watching her as she sucked them inside her mouth, her gaze not leaving his face.

He itched to pick the mango up and re-enact the scene. Cut off thin slices and feed them to Stella one by one. Watch her pupils dilate and her breath become shallow just as Lady Mary's had.

Maybe even hear that whimper again at the back of her throat. The whimper that was all Stella.

Stella's breath hitched as Rick's eyes seemed to suddenly glitter like moonbeams on sapphires. She swallowed her mouthful of mango but juice escaped to her lips and she ran her tongue around them to capture the errant moisture.

Rick shut his eyes and groaned as all his noble intentions from last night faded to black with each revolution of her tongue. 'Stella,' he murmured, his eyelids fluttering open to find her staring at him.

Stella blinked at the ache in his voice. Had he edged closer? Or had she? She looked at his mouth, remembered how it had felt against hers. How it had been so much better than she'd ever fantasised. 'This *is* crazy,' she whispered, mango forgotten.

Rick nodded, his gaze fixed on her mouth, inching his own closer to hers, drawn to her as if she were a homing beacon, his heart rate pulsing to the beat of the sea. 'Certifiable.'

Stella felt his pull as a physical force, which seemed only fitting beneath a canopy of stars with the rhythm of the ocean lulling away the insanity of it all. 'What about the memories, Rick?'

Her voice was low and husky in the quiet of the night as she tried to hang onto the one thing that made sense between them, even though her pulse coursed like an ocean squall through every inch of her body.

Suddenly her mouth felt dry.

So dry.

As if she'd been drinking sea water for days and, not only was her thirst unquenchable, it was sending her slowly mad. She swallowed and licked her lips to ease the dry, parched feeling.

Rick's pupils dilated as her tongue darted out. 'Screw 'em,' he muttered as his final shard of resistance melted away. 'Let's make better ones.'

R-rated ones.

And he closed the distance between them, capturing her mouth. There was a moment, ever so brief, when she could have pulled away, could have protested and he would have been capable of letting it slide. But when she opened to him instantly on a deep-in-his-bones moan the moment passed in a blink of an eye and her mango and coconut essence wrapped him in a sticky web of desire that was impossible to break free of.

Even if he wanted to.

Which he didn't.

His heart crashed in his chest, his breath sawed in and out. Her hands crept around his neck and she made that noise at the back of her throat and somehow, some way, he had her on the deck, her breasts pressed against his chest, her hand shoved in his hair.

Where his beer or her mango had ended up he didn't know and he didn't care. All he knew was she smelled like paradise and felt like every erotic dream he'd ever had, and when she moaned into his mouth her desire tasted sweet like mango and he wanted to devour every drop.

He was hard and needy and something in his head insisted that he touch every inch of her, smell every inch of her, know every inch of her.

His hand drifted south to the wild flutter at the base of her throat and she moaned. It moved further to the top button of her wrap, where the swell of her breast was emphasised by the taut fabric of her bikini top, and she gasped.

It fanned down over her ribs and came to rest on the gentle rise of her belly and she arched her back and undulated her stomach and sighed, 'Yes, yes, yes.'

Rick pulled away, breathing hard. Her face was soft and full of wonder. If he were an egotist he might even have called it rapture.

'Let's go to my cabin,' he murmured, kissing her eyes and the tip of her nose and the corner of her mouth.

Stella opened her lashes, seeing nothing but Rick's face crowned by about a million stars—*when had they come out*?

'No.' She shook her head. 'I want it here, on the deck, beneath the stars.'

She'd wanted to write a similar scene with Vasco and Mary but she'd known that it wouldn't have been possible in the middle of the ocean with a boat full of pirates in the eighteenth century.

But now she got to live the fantasy for real and she wasn't going to have it any other way.

He nuzzled her temple, her ear, her neck. 'Kinky,' he murmured as his hand found its way beneath the hem of her throw to trace patterns on her bare abdomen. The same abdomen that had taunted him all day with its cute little perky belly button.

Stella almost moaned out loud as the buzzing of his lips seemed to stroke other places. Lower places. 'Not into kinky?' she asked, smiling against his mouth as his lips brushed hers.

Rick chuckled as his mouth inched down her throat. 'Kinky is my middle name,' he said as his hand crept inexorably north.

'Really?' Stella said as the possibilities swirled around her mind in a sexual kaleidoscope.

'Really,' he repeated as he pushed her shirt up, pulled aside one bikini bra cup, exposing her breast totally to his view. He smiled as she gasped and the nipple puckered beneath his scrutiny. He stared at it fascinated as his hand groped beside her until he found what he was looking for.

Stella was in a sexual haze so heady she doubted even an undersea earthquake could have shifted her. The way he looked at her nipple as if it were his own private property was utterly mesmerising.

This was Rick. Her Rick. Not a fantasy. Not Vasco Ramirez. Riccardo Granville.

He raised his hand above her chest and it took a few seconds for her to focus on what he was doing, and even then it wasn't until the warm sticky mango juice dripped onto her nipple that his actions registered.

But by then he'd lowered his mouth to it and she'd gasped and arched her back and she knew she was totally lost.

Just as Lady Mary had been.

CHAPTER NINE

Rıck had never tasted anything so sweet as his tongue lapped at the juice, removing every drop from the hard nub. Stella tasted exotic like forbidden fruit, smelled like an ocean breeze riffling through a stand of coconut palms, and the very unladylike expletive that had fallen from her mouth as he nuzzled her breast played like a symphony in his head.

He pulled away and watched as her wet, puckered nipple dried in the breeze. A little frown appeared between her brows just before she moaned a protest and opened her eyes. There was a feverish glitter to her gaze, which went straight to his groin.

He had put that crazy-drunk look there.

The air felt thick and heavy on her palate as Stella dragged in some much-needed breaths. His hand spanned her ribs beneath her breast exactly where her heart pounded like a gong and she wondered if he knew that he had done that to her. He was staring down at her, his gaze roving over her face and chest, lingering on her mouth and her impossibly taut nipple.

'I have another,' she murmured.

Rick smiled. He relieved her of her throw, then smoothed his hand to her other bikini cup and dragged it aside with his index finger, satisfied as her breast spilled free. 'So you do,' he agreed, watching with fascination as the nipple wrinkled then puckered before his eyes. He groped for the discarded mango cheek.

Her pupils dilated and he heard her breath roughen as he squeezed the cheek again and juice dripped onto her breast, coating her nipple and running in sweet rivulets down her chest. His mouth salivated as he inched his head closer to the gloriously sticky morsel. Her low whimper encouraged him to close the distance and he took it greedily instead of repeating the steady assault he'd used on the other side.

She gasped and he sucked harder, rolling the stiff peak around and around his mouth, grazing the tip with his teeth, pressing it hard between palate and tongue, satisfied only when she arched her back, silently begging for more. His hand found the other nipple, hard and ready. When he brushed it with his thumb she panted. And when he pinched it between his fingers she practically levitated off the deck and cried out so loudly he lifted his head and smothered the husky outcry with his mouth.

Stella, driven by a hunger so insatiable she was blind to everything else, lifted her head off the deck and claimed Rick's lips with indecent vigour. She pushed her tongue into his mouth and when he groaned deep and low and needy she swallowed the sound whole, lapping up his response, wanting to fuse their mouths together, to fuse their bodies together for eternity.

Her pulse pounded through her head, her nostrils flared with each laboured breath. His hand left her nipple and stroked down her belly and she shifted restlessly against the deck as muscles deep inside shivered and undulated. The boards were hard against her back but she didn't care. She wanted him on top of her, pressing down, sinking into her. She wanted to feel his skin on hers, wrap her legs around his waist, have the rock and the sway and the pound of them become one with the rhythm of the ocean.

His hand moved lower, whispering across her skin, skimming the edge of her bikini bottoms. Her hips shifted as heat licked from his fingers and bloomed in her pelvis. An ache took up residence between her legs and she moaned as his hand fumbled with a bow.

She felt the tug as he pulled at it and it came undone.

Then another tug as the other bow ceded to his questing fingers and she shivered as he stripped the tiny triangle of fabric away, leaving her bare to the ocean breeze and the stars and his touch.

'Those damn bows have been driving me nuts all day,' Rick said, lifting his head briefly before moving his lips to her jaw, her ear, her throat. And lower, trailing towards her nipple as his fingers slowly stroked her inner thigh.

Stella whimpered as more heat fanned downwards from his kisses and upwards from his hand, searing and ravaging everything in between with devastating ease.

Suddenly it wasn't enough to be just lying here. She wanted to touch his skin—all of it. Feel it smooth and warm and solid beneath her hands, dance fire across it as he was doing to her.

Wreak a little havoc.

Render him a little crazy.

She grabbed for the hem of his shirt, reefing it up and over his head at the exact time his lips met her nipple. She whimpered as he let go for the briefest second and moaned deep and low when his mouth returned immediately to her breast and his fingers found her thigh again. She sucked in a breath, dug her fingernails into the bare warm flesh of his shoulder as he tormented the sensitive peak.

His flesh shuddered beneath her palm and it vibrated all the way down her arm, stroking gossamer fingers over her neck and her chest and down her belly. Her hands kneaded his shoulders and the defined muscles of his back. Her palms smoothed into the dimples she'd seen all those days ago in the moonlight, slipping beneath his waistband to the firm rounded rise of his buttocks.

When he groaned against her mouth she squeezed them hard. Rick reared back as his erection surged painfully, bucking against its confines. 'Stella,' he muttered, seeing stars despite his back being to them.

He recaptured her mouth, plundering its soft sweet depths, getting lost in the taste and the smell and the touch of her. Wanting everything at once, impatient to know the noises she made when she came.

His fingers moved a little north and brushed lightly at the juncture. Her back arched and she cried out as he found her hot and wet and ready. 'God, Stel,' he whispered, his lips hovering above hers. 'You feel so damn good.'

Stella shook her head from side to side, her hips rotating restlessly as his fingers stroked and brushed and sighed against her.

It wasn't enough, she needed more. 'Please,' she whispered.

'Please what?' Rick murmured, licking along the plump softness of her mouth. 'What do you want, Stella?'

Stella arched her back as his finger pressed a little harder, slid through the slick heat of her. 'More,' she said urgently, rotating her hips as she gripped his buttocks convulsively.

Rick slid a finger inside and felt her clamp hard around him. Her gasp echoed around the empty ocean. 'Like this?' he asked, licking down her neck, trailing his tongue down her chest. 'Or this?' He claimed a nipple as he slid another finger home.

'Rick!' Stella clung to him as he stretched her, taunted her. His expert thumb zeroed in on the impossibly hard erogenous zone as if it were fitted with a homing beacon and the stars started to flash in the sky.

A pressure built from deep inside as his thumb fanned and stoked.

God, she was going to come. *Very, very soon.*

'Wait,' she said, removing a hand from his backside to grab his wrist and still his devastatingly rhythmic movements.

Rick lifted his head and frowned. 'What's wrong?' he asked, breathing hard.

If she'd changed her mind, got cold feet, he was toast. He might as well just jump into the ocean now and save himself the slow decline into insanity.

Stella licked her lips. 'It's been a long time,' she panted. 'I swear if you keep doing that it's going to be over very, very quickly.'

It took a moment for her meaning to sink into his lust-addled brain, then everything stopped as he smiled. 'Really? You mean this?' He rotated his fingers deep inside her and grinned at the whimper that rent the air.

'Rick,' she pleaded, squeezing his wrist hard.

'What, Stel?' he murmured. 'You don't like this?' He repeated the manoeuvre, applying pressure to the hard little nub beneath his thumb.

Stella gasped as she shut her eyes. 'Rick, please.'

'What about this?' he asked as he groped awkwardly one-handed for the discarded mango cheek.

Stella opened her eyes as she felt his heat move from her side. His eyes glittered down at her as he half knelt beside her, one hand stroking her intimately, the other paused above the juncture of her thighs.

'You like this, Stella?' he asked as he squeezed the almost spent cheek, wringing the last drops of juice from its now pulpy flesh.

Stella felt the warm sticky ooze mingle with her own slickness as a waft of soft ripe fruit and sex enveloped her. And when he bent over her, his tongue joining the delicious friction, it was too, too much. A sweet wild aroma filled her senses as he stroked and stoked and the pressure accelerated to warp speed.

Rick groaned against her as the salt and the sweet of her slid over his tongue. Her heady aroma surrounded him as he taunted the hard nub, flicking and sucking in equal measure. She bucked and writhed beneath him, begging him to stop,

begging him not to stop, as she lifted her hips in silent sup-
plication.

He pinned her down with his hand and his mouth, lapping
at her sweetness, refusing to yield. Even when she shattered
around him seconds later he gave more, wringing every last
tantalising morsel from her as he had done with the mango.

Stella jackknifed up, crying out, 'Stop, stop, stop,' fearing
that she might actually die from the intensity of the pleasure.

Rick was breathing hard as he withdrew, rocking back
on his haunches, watching as Stella collapsed back against
the deck, delightfully naked aside from two pushed-aside bra
cups.

He quirked an eyebrow. 'You look like you needed that.'

Stella grunted, which was all she was capable of as strong
post-coital aftershocks undulated deep inside her. The stars
burst around her like fireworks. 'You have no idea,' she panted.

Diana would be proud.

He ran his eyes over her naked abandon one more time. She
lay all loose limbed, her nipples still erect, her legs spread, and
his erection twitched painfully in his boardies. 'I think I do.'

Stella saw a flash of carnal hunger glitter in his eyes, aware
suddenly that she'd short-changed him. 'I'm sorry,' she said,
her breath still laboured. 'I don't know what the equivalent
of premature ejaculation is in females but I think I just had
an acute attack.'

Rick chuckled. 'It was my pleasure.' He held out his hand
to her and pulled her towards him as she took it, kissing her
nose. 'Fancy a shower?'

Stella was pleased for the cover of night as an image of a
naked Rick, water and moonlight caressing his magnificent
body, sprang instantly to mind. Never, all those nights ago
when she'd spied on him, had she thought she'd ever be joining him under the deck shower.

He didn't give her a chance to indulge the embarrassing
memory or to say no, pulling her to her feet, dragging her to-

wards the bow. He let go of her to flick on the taps and rip at the Velcro on his boardies. In a trice they were gone and he was standing before her, proud and erect, the jut of his sex a tantalising silhouette. An illicit reminder of her peep show with the full embellishment of her fantasy life included for good measure.

Rick felt a tug deep inside as she stared at his erection. Somewhere behind him the water sprayed unattended, his heart pounding just as erratically. The moisture in his mouth dried to dust. 'Your turn,' he murmured.

She frowned for a moment, confused by his comment, then she looked down at her half-on, half-off bikini top and understood. She pulled it off over her head, being careful not to jar her almost recovered arm. It dropped to the deck next to his boardies.

Rick devoured her curvy roundness in one long slow look. 'You're beautiful,' he breathed.

'So are you,' she murmured, her gaze roaming over the perfection of him. This was how she had imagined Vasco. But Rick was more. So much more. He was no figment of her imagination. He was solid flesh and hard muscle and warm blood and he wanted her—*Stella*—not Mary.

She hadn't even realised she'd been jealous of Mary until this moment.

But then Rick held out his hand again and she took it and everything else was forgotten. He stepped backwards into the shower and she followed, watching as the water soaked his hair and ran down his chest, before running free down his obliques.

She stepped closer, raising herself on tippy toe, gliding her hands up his pecs and onto his shoulders. His erection pushed against her belly, thick and rampant, and her hand reached for it as she lifted her mouth to his. She felt the jolt through his body as she palmed the length of him and swallowed his groan as their lips fused.

'Oh…dear…God,' Rick gasped against her mouth as she

increased the intensity of her intimate caress, using the water to her advantage.

Stella couldn't agree with his sentiments more. She could taste mango and sex on his mouth and the water flowing over their heated skin caressed like icicles and he felt good and right in her hand.

But she wanted him good and right elsewhere.

Inside her.

Deep, deep inside her.

'You need to be in me,' she panted, her pulse thrumming so loudly through her ears she was sure she was about to rupture her eardrums.

Rick didn't need a written invitation. He grabbed her around the waist, boosting her up. As she locked her ankles at his waist he turned around in one easy movement. He pushed her against the entirely inadequate pole the shower head was mounted upon and lowered his mouth to hers, plundering hers until nothing but their two frantic heartbeats registered.

Not even the push and pull of the vast, vast ocean.

And when that wasn't enough he dropped his head to her chest, devouring the delicious ripeness of her breasts, revelling in the arch of her back and the crazed keening coming from her throat.

'Now,' Stella begged, her head thrown back, her chest thrust out in pure debauched abandon.

Rick was hard and ready and done with denying himself. He lifted her slightly, aligning her, aligning himself, nudging her entrance, feeling the still slick heat of her.

'Rick!' she begged, lightly pummelling a fist against the muscles of his shoulder as she felt him thick and hard but still not where she wanted him.

Where she needed him.

Rick chuckled at her frustration. 'Easy, Stel, easy. Let's make it last this time, huh?'

Stella whacked him harder. '*Now*, damn it,' she ordered.

Rick grinned. 'Aye, aye captain,' he murmured, smothering the very unladylike bellow that came from her mouth as he pushed into her long and hard and deep.

Stella broke away, gasping for air as he slowly withdrew and steadily pushed his way back in again, hitting exactly the right spot every time. 'Oh, God, yes,' she panted. 'Just there. Don't stop. God, don't stop!'

She squirmed against him, her head lolling back, water flowing down her breasts, her lips parting in a blissful O.

Rick stroked his tongue down her throat, sipping at the rivulets of water as he kept up the slow easy pace. Her whimpers vibrated against his mouth and he pushed deeper as he slowed right down.

Stella moaned as the subtle friction drove her crazy.

In a good way.

In a never-ever-stop way.

The way she'd always imagined it.

Hard and slow and perfect.

But this was better. So much better. Because it was real.

Rick watched Stella's breasts rock as he slowly surged into her again. Water sluiced down her chest, traced the contours of her cleavage, clung in droplets at the ends of her nipples. Stars formed a crown above her head and with her blonde hair plastered in wet strips over her shoulders she looked like a water nymph.

'God,' Rick groaned, his forehead falling against her chest as the tightness in his groin started to tug at his resistance. 'You look great in a shower.'

Stella gasped as he pulled out further this time and thrust all the way in. *So did he.* 'I have a confession,' she murmured.

Rick felt his orgasm drawing nearer and beat it back. 'You do?' he panted.

She nodded as his pulsing became thrusting once again. 'When you had a shower the other night at the yacht club in

Moresby…' her teeth sank into her lower lip and she clenched his shoulder as he picked up the pace '…I was spying on you.'

Rick pulled out all the way this time, pushing back in until she gasped and arched her back. He was a perfect fit.

'I have a confession too,' he said as a more urgent rhythm took over, nudging the slow inexorable build into something much harder to control. He withdrew quickly and just as quickly plunged back in. 'I saw you.'

If she hadn't been about to come Stella might have been angry. *Embarrassed certainly.* But the fact that he'd known, that he'd turned so she could see all of him, was inexplicably arousing. That combined with the continual in-and-out thrust of him was a heady combination.

'Pervert,' she gasped as he hit the spot that made her shudder and quiver and cling.

Rick grunted as her fingernails dug in and everything started to unravel. 'Look who you're calling pervert, my lovely.'

Stella was going to say something else, but all that came out was a gurgly whimper as she let the hypocritical protest fly up and become stardust. 'Ah-h-h,' she cried out as time and space blurred and all that remained was him and her and the silent permission of the ocean.

Rick felt things heat and boil as his belly tensed to an unbearable rigidity. He pulled her into him and crooned, 'Yes, Stella, yes,' directly into her ear as she threw back her head and called out his name, clamping tight around him, falling apart in his arms.

It was all that he needed and he bellowed into her chest, thrusting with none of the finesse of earlier as he rode the savage dictates of his body to their final release.

After a long night of getting acquainted in a way they never had before, Stella woke late the next morning to find Rick propped up on his elbow looking down at her. His eyes seemed even bluer in the morning sunshine slanting through his undressed portholes, his eyelashes longer. His hair seemed shaggier as it hung around his face and brushed his broad bronzed shoulders. His lips fuller.

He should look girly but he didn't.

He looked utterly masculine with nothing but a white sheet riding low on his hips.

'Good morning,' she murmured, blushing as she remembered just what lay beneath that sheet and the things he'd done with it.

She'd done with it.

Rick smiled at the pinkness in her cheeks, surprised that someone who knew him so carnally was capable of such modesty. 'Good morning to you too,' he replied, dropping a kiss on a bare shoulder.

His smile slackened as a feeling he wasn't familiar with washed over him and took up residence in his gut like a lead sinker. Nothing like how he usually felt the morning after—loose and light with all his kinks ironed out. Stella wasn't some bar hook-up or one of his many port calls. He wasn't sure what came next.

Stella noted his pensive look. 'I hope that's not buyer's remorse,' she murmured.

Rick shook his head. If she slapped him in the face and swam back home to England right this moment and refused to see him again he would never regret last night. 'Never.'

He lowered his head again and kissed her on the mouth, a long, slow, lingering kiss that tasted of them and left him hard beneath the sheet and aching for more.

Stella sighed as he pulled back, brushing her fingers along the soft bristles of his perpetual three day growth. 'So what's up?' she murmured.

He turned his face, kissing the tips of her fingers. 'I guess,' he said, looking down into her sleepy olive gaze, 'I'm not sure what comes next…'

Stella smiled. 'Breakfast, I think. Unless you want to—' she dropped her hand to his chest, traced her index finger down his belly to the interesting bulge in the sheet '—fool around a bit more?'

Rick captured her hand before it hit her target and thinking wouldn't be possible. 'Stel,' he said. 'I'm serious. Normally I'd kiss you and tell you I had to be somewhere in a couple of hours but…this is you and…I don't have a well-rehearsed morning-after plan for this. Frankly I'm torn between freaking out and ringing Andy Willis to tell him I've seen your boobs.'

Stella laughed, letting her hand fall to the mattress. Andy Willis had been Rick's best friend when he'd been eleven and had spent a couple of weeks one summer on the *Persephone* with them. He'd also had a massive crush on Stella.

Rick frowned down at her. 'It's not funny, Stella.'

Stella sobered, finding his pout irresistible. She lifted her head to kiss it away. He resisted until she tugged on his bottom lip with her teeth and soothed it with her tongue. She smiled when he groaned and kissed her back.

She pulled away when they were both breathing hard, smoothing his brow with her thumb.

'You're not eleven any more, Rick. What's happened with us has taken us both by surprise so I don't have a plan for this either. But do we really need one?'

She remembered what Diana had said—*you're going to be on that boat with him for long periods of time where there'll be nothing to do*. She'd rejected it then as an impossibility but, after last night, maybe Diana had a point.

'You and I both know that we live two very different lives and also know through the bitter experience of two broken families that they're practically mutually exclusive. But for the next little while we're on this boat together—alone—and we're both single and of age and if last night is any yardstick, we're pretty damn good together. Can't that be our plan?'

Rick thought it sounded like possibly the best ever plan

he'd heard. But could things really be that simple between the two of them? If he shut his eyes he could hear Nathan telling him how special Stella was, what she deserved out of life. And what she didn't.

'I don't know, Stel, maybe your father was right—'

Stella shook her head vigorously, interrupting him, annoyed that her father had meddled to the extent he had. She'd always wondered why none of her father's crew had ever spent much time with her once she'd grown breasts and now she knew.

'No, he was wrong. About a *lot* of things but especially this. I understand, Rick. You're like him. I get it. The ocean runs in your veins and the sea is your mistress blah blah.'

She rolled her eyes.

'And I want marriage and one day babies and for the father of those babies to be around full time. I know all that. But that's not what this is. We're not talking marriage and happily-ever-afters here, Rick. We're talking a couple of weeks of hot, sweaty, sandy, frolicking-in-tropical-lagoons sex.'

Rick shut his eyes against the images she evoked as his hard-on voted yes. But...he looked down at her, her blonde hair spread out on the pillow around her, her lovely face so, so familiar...could a woman who immersed herself in happily-ever-afters ever settle for less?

'And then what? We just go back to being friends?'

Stella shrugged. 'Sure. It's not like we see each other much these days, Rick. What...two or three times a year? Probably even less now that Dad's not around. Hell, it'll probably be another year or so before I next see you.'

Rick had to admit she made a good point. 'That's true,' he murmured.

Stella smiled, her hand making its way back to where the sheet still bulged interestingly. 'The truth, the whole truth and nothing but the truth.'

Rick dropped his head to nuzzle along her collarbone. 'It certainly makes sense.'

Her hand dipped under the sheet and she hit pay dirt. Rick swore in Spanish, and she smiled, recognising the word he had taught her when she'd been twelve years old. She wrapped her palm around his girth and revelled in the silky hard length of him and the way he shuddered against her.

She stretched languorously, her free hand slipping under the pillow, grabbing a fistful of sheet as Rick claimed a nipple, sucking it into the heat of his mouth, lashing it with hot wet swipes of his tongue.

Her hand nudged something and it took her lust-drunk brain a moment to ascertain it was a book. Without thinking she pulled it out and looked at it.

The cover of *Pleasure Hunt* stared back at her.

She said a choice swear word of her own, snagging Rick's attention.

'Ah...' he said warily.

'You've read this?'

She frowned as he collapsed back on the mattress and nodded, her worst fears confirmed. She'd wondered when they'd first had that conversation about her writing process if he'd read it, but his comments had set her mind at ease.

His obviously misleading comments.

'This is Diana's copy,' she said as she thumbed through it. She'd have known it without the benefit of her autograph on the title page. She'd know this dog-eared copy anywhere— she'd seen Diana reading it often enough.

'Yes. She gave it to me just before we left your house that day.'

'Oh, did she, now?' Stella murmured, her ire rising as she formulated a rather stinging email rant in her head. But then another thought hit and she sat bolt upright. 'Oh, God,' she said as the most important thing of all occurred to her. She turned her head and looked down at him. 'So you know...'

She couldn't even finish the statement, it was so embarrassing.

Rick grinned at her mortified look as he crossed his ankles and clasped his hands behind his head. 'That I'm Vasco Ramirez?'

The pink she'd gone earlier was nothing to the deep red that currently suffused her cheeks. She opened her mouth to deny it but she couldn't. If he'd read it, he'd know. There was too much of *him* in it. Not just that tantalising birthmark but the essence of him. His mannerisms, his way with words, his sense of humour.

His sense of honour.

She looked away, her fingers absently stroking the raised lettering on the cover. 'Well, there's no need to get too bigheaded about it,' she huffed. 'I needed a pirate of Spanish descent. It made sense to…model him on someone I knew.'

Whatever happened she couldn't let him know that she'd been fantasising about him for a long time before Vasco had come on the scene. That Vasco had walked into her head fully formed because of him. He was already freaked out enough about the development in their relationship.

'But any resemblance to person or persons alive or dead…'

Rick vaulted upright, fitting himself in behind her, his front to her back, covering her mouth with his hand, cutting off the lawyer speak as he kissed her shoulder. 'Shh, Stella,' he murmured. 'I love it that you *modelled* him on me.'

He brushed a string of kisses up higher as he dropped his hand to her shoulder. 'I'm not going to sue you, I'm…flattered. And impressed how…accurate…' he smiled against her skin '…your descriptions are. That bath scene…' He nuzzled her ear; his hands moved to cup her breasts, his thumbs brushing over the already erect nipples. 'It was like you'd painted a portrait of me.'

Stella arched her back and felt her eyes roll back in her head as his mouth and fingers turned her insides to mush.

Rick kissed up her jaw and when she turned her head towards him he feathered kisses along her lips. 'Like you'd actually seen me naked,' he whispered against her mouth as one hand left her breast bearing south.

His words triggered a thought and Stella opened her eyes. 'You knew,' she murmured. 'You'd already read the book when you spied me watching you have that shower.'

He chuckled unashamedly in her ear as both hands stroked her thighs. 'Guilty,' he whispered.

Her brow wrinkled as she remembered how cannily familiar some things on this trip had been. The shower incident. When he'd tended her wounds as Vasco had done. When he'd squeezed mango juice all over her body.

But he'd turned her whole body into an erogenous zone and when he urged her thighs apart she didn't object.

'Have you been deliberately enacting scenes from the book?' she murmured, raising both arms and linking them around his neck, arching her back as his finger slid between her legs.

'What did you expect me to do for fun when you took away all my recreational flirting? Anyway, do you care?' he whispered, his erection pressing into the cleft of her soft round buttocks.

'Yes,' she sighed. 'I'm mad as he...ll.' And she would have sounded much more convincing had he not driven a finger deep inside her.

He chuckled at her breathy whimper. 'Are you telling me you haven't been taking advantage too? That you didn't think about the book when you were spying on me in the shower? Or when I was tending to your wounds? That bringing those scenes to life didn't excite you?'

Stella knew he was right. Knew that it would be hard to take the moral high ground when she'd been using him to indulge a few of her own fantasies.

But she was damned if she was going to let him have it all his way. 'It's just a story,' she panted as he stroked between her legs. 'They're what excited Lady Mary.'

Rick remembered what she'd said about Lady Mary not being her in anything other than a generic female way. Her slickness coated his fingers and he picked up the pace. 'And you're not her, right?' he whispered.

Stella was so close to falling over the edge. So far gone she didn't know which way was up, but even she knew to answer that question truthfully would be madness.

'Right,' she gasped as she squirmed against him and he stroked harder.

She clutched convulsively at the back of his neck as a tiny pulse fluttered deep and low, fanning out in ever-increasing waves. Mary was forgotten, Vasco was forgotten as it pulsed and grew until nothing else mattered but the magic Rick could do with his hands.

'Oh, God,' she groaned, arching her back, tilting her pelvis. 'Don't stop,' she begged. 'Please don't stop.'

Rick felt the tension in his groin tighten to almost unbearable tautness. 'Yes, Stel, yes,' he panted, working her slickness, feeling her ripple around him. 'Come for me. Come.'

Stella bucked as the wave broke over her, undulating with a ferocity that tore the breath from her lungs and, for a moment or two, the beat from her heart.

It gripped her and shook her in endless waves and she knew there was no possible way she could be put back together right, once it ended.

CHAPTER TEN

Mary chafed against the four silken bonds that imprisoned her, legs akimbo, upon Vasco's bed. For no matter how many times she shared it with him she would never regard it as hers. She eyed the big brooding pirate as he prowled back and forth. He was wearing breeches and boots and nothing else save the sunlight slanting through the portholes.

He stopped and turned to face her from the foot of the bed, shoving his hands on his hips. 'I'm waiting, Mary.'

His low rumble set her heart aflutter and her nipples to attention. She watched as his glittering blue eyes took in their state of indecency. How could they not when she was barely covered? When he had stripped her to her undergarments not ten minutes ago this had not been the expected outcome.

Damned stubborn man.

'I insist that you untie me immediately, Captain Ramirez.'

Vasco chuckled, his gaze fanning over the hard peaks tenting her chemise. 'Methinks you like to be tied up, Lady Mary,' he murmured, planting a knee on the bed.

She glared at him both scandalised and titillated at the thought. 'Captain Ramirez.'

He ignored the warning in her voice, slowly advancing onto the bed. 'I do so prefer it when you call me Vasco. Like you did that day on the deck when I washed your hair.' He prowled closer on his hands and knees until he was sitting on his haunches between her spreadeagled legs. 'And when I first touched you here,' he murmured, stroking his finger down the open central seam of her linen drawers.

She sucked in a breath and he smiled triumphantly. 'Like you did last night and the night before that and the five nights before that.' He stroked again.

Mary squirmed against his hand. 'Vasco, please,' she moaned. 'It's the middle of the day. The crew...'

He shook his head and chuckled that she could still keep a sense of propriety while tied to his bed. 'Say it,' he insisted. 'If you want it, Mary, you're going to have to ask for it.'

Lady Mary Bingham had been a willing and eager bed partner but there was part of her he hadn't been able to reach, a part she kept aloof from him even when she was in the throes of her release. It made him feel like a common street urchin and she the lady who was condescending to allow him to use her body while she had nothing better to do.

He needed to know that this fever was burning in her blood too.

Mary shook her head. Gently bred ladies did not talk so.

She'd already taken a pirate as a lover. How much more did he want? 'I will not.'

Vasco smiled at her, watching as she bit down on her bottom lip and fought against closing her eyes. 'You know you want to, Mary, I can feel it right here...' He slipped a finger inside her where it was hot and slick and she gasped. 'I know you, Mary.'

Mary hated how he could addle her senses so quickly.

'You know nothing about me, sir,' she said vehemently as her hips moved against him restlessly.

Vasco grinned. 'I know you like this,' he said, pushing up her chemise with his other hand, exposing a creamy breast and rosy nipple that puckered quickly beneath the stroke of his fingers.

'I know you have this tiny strawberry birthmark just here,' he said, satisfied to hear her whimper as he withdrew his finger, shifting it slightly to the left to the crease where her inner thigh met the very centre of her. 'I know you like it when I lick you there,' he murmured, lowering his head and putting his tongue to where his finger had been, to the mark that had fascinated him right from the beginning.

'Vasco...' Mary cried, arching her back as his finger re-entered her and his tongue swiped in long, lazy, knowing strokes.

He smiled as he pulled away, sitting back on his haunches, his finger still stroking deep inside her. 'I know me tying you up excites you even though I know you're hearing your uncle's voice telling you you're going to hell.'

Mary also hated how he seemed to be able to read her mind. 'Well, I'll be seeing you there first, Captain Ramirez,' she said haughtily.

Vasco threw back his head and laughed. When he stopped his eyes glittered down at her and he started to stroke her in earnest. 'Ah, but what a way to go, Lady Mary,' he taunted as he relentlessly increased the pressure.

Mary especially hated how he could bring her to her peak so effortlessly. 'Vasco,' she whimpered and moved against him, desperate for the rush.

He quirked an eyebrow, easing back a little, refusing to give her what she craved. If she wanted to use him *then she could damn well say the words. 'Yes, Mary, what do you want?'*

Mary rocked her pelvis against his hand as the maddening friction plateaued, divinity frustratingly out of reach. 'Please, Vasco,' she gasped.

Vasco was harder than he'd ever been in his life, watching her lying before him half exposed, fully abandoned, head tossing from side to side, her body begging for that which she would not put into words.

He shook his head. 'Please what, Mary?' he demanded, quickening the pace for a few tantalising seconds, then backing off.

Mary bit into her lip hard, lifting her hips off the bed. 'Vasco!'

'Say it,' he growled.

She opened her eyes and glared at him. 'Damn it, Vasco.' But she knew in that second she'd have given him the world if he'd asked for it. 'I like it when you do this to me,' she said. 'I want you to do it to me. I just plain want you. Now please...please...' her wrists yanked at the bonds '...I beg of you...'

Vasco grinned. 'Of course, Lady Mary, why didn't you just say so?'

But the rebuke that came to Mary's lips was lost as Vasco drove her over the edge in ten seconds. When she was capable of opening her eyes a little while later it was to his smug triumphant smile.

'Okay, Vasco,' she said, her breathing still not quite normal. 'Untie me now.'

Vasco shook his head and the gleam in his eye was positively wicked as he unlaced his breeches.

'I'm just getting started.'

THE next week flew by. Between long nights—and sometimes long days—below deck they made it to Micronesia, sailing into Weno in Chuuk State where they restocked and sorted out the official paperwork.

Chuuk, home to a giant lagoon, the final resting place for over a hundred ships, planes and submarines that had perished during fierce World War Two battles, was a magnate for wreck divers worldwide. Time and warm tropical waters had seen the wrecks bloom into breathtaking coral gardens and artificial reefs sporting a kaleidoscope of colours.

But they headed beyond that to the lesser known outer reefs fringing the deeper waters of the Pacific where Nathan had been convinced Inigo's boat had gone down in bad weather. The islands of Micronesia had once been part of the Spanish East Indies and, Nathan believed, a rich hunting ground for a pirate who wasn't picky or patriotic when it came to loot.

The fact that a veritable maze of two thousand plus, mainly uninhabited islands lay at his disposal, providing the perfect cover to lay low in between raids, had no doubt also been a plus for Inigo Alvarez.

The weather stayed calm and visibility was excellent as, for the first six days, Rick and Stella island-hopped, diving the area Nathan had deduced from his lifetime of research was the most likely resting pace for *The Mermaid*. It was about a hundred nautical miles square so they divided it up into a grid and painstakingly explored each segment from sun up to sundown.

Had they been in the *Persephone* or one of the other boats in the salvage fleet, they would have had all kinds of equipment to help them in their quest. But this was just a basic exploratory—old-fashioned treasure hunting at its best. Like they were kids again, pretending to find Spanish galleons while their fathers undertook their latest salvage operation.

And neither of them would have had it any other way.

The deepest water was ten metres but it still took a couple of dives for Stella to gain her confidence. Ever since she could swim, Stella had dived, and she'd held her open water diving certification for many years, but she hadn't been in a wetsuit for some time now.

Rick, used to diving much, much deeper, enjoyed the slower pace and took time to admire the magnificent underwater scenery, including the curvy little water nymph in a wetsuit that left nothing to the imagination.

At night she wrote, more inspired than ever by being back in the water again, and he reviewed the data from their dives.

And then they burned up the sheets.

On the seventh day they rested. They anchored off one of the many sandy atolls, loaded up the dinghy and motored the short distance, beaching the little runabout high above the tide level. They lolled in the shallows, making love as the water lapped gently around their legs. They sunbathed nude and ate sandwiches and drank cold beer for lunch. They dozed under a stand of coconut palms.

Three other islands could be seen nearby, towering out of the glittering ocean, and in the distance another boat, probably a dive charter, slowly traversed the horizon. It was a reminder that they weren't the only two people in the world, which had been an easy assumption to make these last idyllic days.

'Maybe we could just move here?' Stella said sleepily.

Rick smiled as he rolled his head to look at her. 'Sounds good to me.' If he was going to be stuck on a deserted island with anyone, she would be his preference. 'What happens when the laptop runs out of battery?' he teased.

Stella smiled too. 'Don't be practical,' she murmured as she drifted off again.

When she woke the sun wasn't as high overhead and Rick was lying on his stomach propped up on his elbows beside her. A sea breeze ruffled the papers he was reading. She lay there for a few minutes listening to the swish of the waves against the beach and the rustle of the wind through the palm leaves.

I could get used to this.

She rolled up onto her elbow, dropping a kiss on his bare

shoulder. 'What if it's not here?' she asked. 'What if *The Mermaid* is like Atlantis or El Dorado?'

Rick turned his head and nuzzled her temple before returning his attention to the research material he'd printed off the web just prior to leaving the boat this morning. He'd pored over everything he could get his hands on since deciding to undertake this voyage and he'd come across some more potentially useful information last night.

'It might not be here but I think your father's research definitely supports its existence and his reasonings for *The Mermaid* being in these waters are very sound.'

Stella nodded. She hoped so. It would be good to know that something her father had committed so much of his time and energy to might be realised. They'd both been aware, subliminally, that this voyage had been a pilgrimage of sorts. A way to pay homage to Nathan and his dream.

Neither of them wanted to return empty-handed.

'I'm going for a snorkel,' she said. 'You want to join me?'

Rick shook his head. 'Maybe later.'

Stella kissed his shoulder again. 'Are you sure?' she asked. 'I'm going naked.'

Ah, now that got his attention.

He smiled at her before kissing her hard on the mouth. 'Temptress,' he muttered as he pulled away. 'Be off with you.'

Stella laughed. 'Okay, fine,' she said, standing and stripping off her bikini where she stood, throwing it down on the papers he was reading.

Rick chuckled as he picked it up and looked over his shoulder to find her naked, hips swaying seductively as she sashayed down to the shoreline, a mask and snorkel in one hand. Her skin was a light golden brown from all the sun she'd been getting and as she turned and gave him a wave he copped a magnificent side view of full breast and tiny waist before she waded into the ocean. He levered himself up, turning to sit, papers still in hand, watching as the warm tropical waters slowly swallowed her up.

He realised after looking up for the tenth time in ten minutes he was too distracted to read. The reef was close to the shore so she was only a couple of metres out and he could see the bobbing of her naked bottom as she lazily circled back and forth across the surface, occasionally duck diving and blowing water out of her snorkel when she reappeared.

When a coconut fell beside him, missing him by about an inch, he decided it was time to give up and just enjoy the view. He absently picked up the coconut and shook it, hearing the swish of milk inside. He grabbed his diver's knife out of his backpack and, being an old hand at husking coconuts, quickly did so.

By the time the outer shell was peeled away and he'd removed the stringy bark, revealing the hard smooth surface, Stella was emerging from the ocean like something from a James Bond film.

Except nude. Her blonde hair slicked back from her face, clinging to her naked back like a sheath of honey-gold silk.

Like a mermaid.

He brought the bald nut to his face and inhaled the sweet earthy aroma as he watched her walking towards him. The fragrance was pure Stella.

A fragrance he'd become quite addicted to.

Her bell tinkled as she drew closer, his erection increasing with her every footfall. When she threw the snorkel and mask down beside him his mouth was as dry as the powdery sand beneath him.

'Do women practise that little hip swing or is it just part of their DNA?' he asked, looking up into her face. Water droplets clung to her eyelashes and ran down her body.

Stella laughed as she deliberately reached behind her to wrap her hair around her hand and squeeze out the excess water. 'I don't know what you're talking about.' She grinned.

'Oh, yeah?' he growled as he threw the coconut down and gently tumbled her to the ground.

Stella went down laughing, clinging to his shoulders as she settled against the soft sand. He straddled her, looming above. The grains felt warm and powdery beneath the cool skin of her back, as did the sun on her face, their formerly shaded position now mostly in light as the day grew later.

'I'm going to have sand everywhere,' she grouched good-naturedly.

'That's the plan.' He grinned as he lowered his mouth to hers. Her lips and the curve of her waist were cool to touch. 'Water cold?' he asked as his tongue lapped at the water droplets still clinging and cooling her throat.

Stella shut her eyes and angled her neck to give him wider access. 'A little.'

Rick smiled against her neck. He sat and groped around beside him. 'Let's see if we can't warm you up.'

Stella opened her eyes just in time to see him holding a coconut and his diver's knife over her abdomen. As a teenager she'd often watched him husk a coconut, the muscles of his back and arms way more fascinating than they should have been.

She quirked an eyebrow. 'Been busy?'

He grinned as he struck the coconut with the handle of the knife right between the eyes. It capitulated easily, cracking in half, clear fluid running out over his hand and dripping onto her cool belly.

He eased it apart, gratified to hear her gasp as he poured most of the warm milk over her belly and breasts. Her nipples ruched before him and his erection surged. He groaned as the aroma of ocean and her wafted up to him and he bent his head to her.

'I want to taste you here,' he muttered. His hot tongue swiped over puckered nipples and she arched her back. He removed every trace of the warm juice before moving on.

'And here,' he said, going down, following the trail of liquid that had puddled in her belly button. He heard the suck of her breath as he lapped it up. She tasted sweet and salty. Like the ocean, tropical breezes and the soft sugary nirvana of coconuts.

He sat back on his haunches, watching her, waiting for her to open her eyes. When her eyelashes fluttered open he picked up the half-coconut that still had a little milk remaining.

'And here,' he murmured, trickling it between her legs, as he had done with the mango, supressing a groan as she licked her lips and panted, her thighs parting, the sunlight glistening there so he could see it coating all of her.

He tossed the shell aside, swooping his head down, his hands gliding up her body to cup her breasts, his thumbs brushing across the nipples.

It was then, as he used his elbows to push her open to him more, that he noticed it for the first time. The sun shone like a spotlight and it was suddenly obvious.

A tiny blemish. A pink birthmark.

Exactly where Lady Mary had hers.

He stared at it, as he tried to think past the pounding of his heart.

So...she was Lady Mary?

But the heady aroma of her drowned in coconut juice was rendering his thought processes useless. He wanted to ask her. Needed to know.

He should stop and demand that she tell him the truth.

But she was making those little noises at the back of her throat again and as another waft of coconut headed his way he actually salivated.

Stella rotated her pelvis as the anticipation built to breaking point. Rick liked to tease but this had gone on long enough. She knew the touch of his mouth was coming and every second he made her wait, she could feel herself get wetter.

'Rick!' she begged, unable to bear it any longer. 'Please,' she whimpered, lifting her hips involuntarily. 'Please.'

It was the whimper that did it—just as it always did. There would be time enough for questions later. So he shut his eyes and gave her what she was asking for, licking that cute strawberry mark just as Vasco had done, savouring the sweet coconut essence of her, pinning her to the sand with his tongue and not letting her up until her climax rent the air.

Stella woke the next morning to a tight feeling at her wrists and a strange sense of foreboding. It was immediately allayed when she saw Rick, one knee planted on the edge of the mattress, his face hovering over her, smiling.

'Morning,' he murmured, kissing her.

She kissed him back. It wasn't until she tried to move her arms to hug him that the foreboding returned. It only took a moment to figure out why. She looked behind her. Her wrists were tied with some kind of material to the posts of his bed. As were her feet.

She was naked and spreadeagled.

Her pulse leapt at the illicitness of it all. Was Rick going to enact the scene from *Pleasure Hunt* where Vasco had tied Mary to the bed?

She looked at him. 'You do know that, unlike Mary, I am perfectly willing to ask you for sex and, not only that, but to tell you how, when, where and the number of times I want you to do me, right?'

Rick chuckled as he sat on the edge of the bed. 'I've noticed. You're really not her, are you?' he asked innocently.

Stella nodded as she averted her eyes to her ankle ties. 'Is that one of my sarongs?' she asked.

Rick grinned. 'Sorry. I'm all out of eighteenth-century satin sashes and I thought it'd be gentler on your wrists and ankles than nautical rope.'

Stella pulled against the bonds to test them and had to

agree. Even if she wanted to get out of them, which she didn't, she knew it would be futile—sailors knew how to tie knots.

'How on earth did you manage not to wake me?' she asked.

He shrugged. 'Well, it took me a while and, thankfully, you're a heavy sleeper.'

Stella nodded. That was true. 'So, was there a purpose to this or are you just into bondage suddenly?'

Rick looked at her, naked and spread on his bed like a gift from Neptune himself. He was ragingly hard and pleased he'd decided to put on some boardies instead of being naked as he'd originally thought yesterday when he'd lain in post-coital glory on the beach beside her, formulating this plan to get a confession out of her.

He wasn't sure why knowing whether she was Lady Mary was increasingly important to him.

It just was.

He'd often wondered if she thought about him. Knowing that she might have fantasised about *them* while he'd been training himself not to was beyond tantalising. Maybe it was ego, maybe it was something else he didn't want to examine too closely, but he had to know.

And he'd known that there was only one way to find out.

He smiled down at her as he pushed off his bed. 'Oh, there's a purpose.'

Stella's nipples hardened beneath his incendiary blue gaze as she noticed she was the only one naked. 'You're dressed.' She pouted.

His smile broadened. 'For now.'

Stella's heart beat a little faster at the promise in those two incredible eyes the exact colour of the tropical waters surrounding them.

Rick prowled around the bed as Vasco had done, his gaze boldly running over every delectable inch of her. Blatantly lingering on her breasts and the strawberry mark he couldn't see from this distance but he knew the exact location of—low and to the left of her centre. Their gazes locked as he roamed, dragging out the moment.

He stopped at the foot of the bed, shoving his hands on his hips. 'I discovered something very interesting yesterday,' he murmured.

The timbre of his voice dragged silken fingers across her skin. 'Really?' She hoped she sounded nonchalant, that the vibration of her madly fluttering heart wasn't shaking the entire bed.

He nodded as he planted a knee on the mattress. 'It's intriguing to say the least,' he continued.

'Something to do with Inigo?' she asked as she watched Rick prowl towards her, the light of a fictional pirate in his eyes.

He shook his head. 'No. Something to do with you.'

'Oh?' Her voice sounded high and breathy as he came right in close, his knees brushing her spread inner thighs.

Rick reached out and brushed his fingertips down her exposed centre. Stella gasped and bucked. He smiled. 'You like that, don't you?'

Stella bit her lip and nodded her head as the brush became something more purposeful. 'Yes.'

The hammer of his heart was loud in his head as his finger followed the path of her heat and sank inside her. 'And this?'

Stella whimpered. 'Yes.'

'You want more?' he asked, sliding another finger home, using his thumb to rub the spot that was already tight and hard.

Stella was ready in an instant, balanced on a knife edge of anticipation. 'Yes.'

Rick smiled. 'Don't you want to know what I discovered?'

She arched her back as he picked up the pace. 'Yes, yes.'

Rick swallowed. She looked so bloody desirable at the mercy of his hand that he wanted to rip his boardies off and forget the damn birthmark but it was about more than the blemish.

Had she ever fantasised about them together? As he had despite Nathan's unspoken law? Had she felt something more than friendship for him?

As he had.

He had to know.

He withdrew his fingers from inside her. 'I found that you, too, have a birthmark.'

Stella felt her orgasm recede beyond her reach as her breath stuttered to a halt. She opened her eyes to find his blue ones glittering down at her.

'Strangely enough,' he continued, sliding his finger to the left, locating the blemish immediately, 'in exactly the same spot that Lady Mary has hers. Coincidence, Stel, or are *you* Lady Mary?'

She shook her head vigorously. *This was not what she'd expected.* 'No.'

What would he think if he knew? He'd already guessed too much about her fantasy life from *Pleasure Hunt*.

He quirked an eyebrow as he brushed his finger against the birthmark again. 'Really?'

Stella panted even as she fought not to. 'Really.'

He moved his hand from her completely. 'I think you're lying, Stella. Mary's so very, very familiar to me.'

It was something he'd only just realised, too caught up in the big things to recognise the subtleties of the character. The nuances. The jut of her chin, the turn of her head, the glimpse of her humanity beneath all her starched upper-class Britishness.

Stella glared at him, now torn between telling him to go to hell and lying to him so he'd finish what he'd started.

And she felt vulnerable.

A state that had nothing to do with her nudity.

He wanted her to look at things that she'd never questioned too deeply.

'What the hell does it matter?' she asked in exasperation, yanking against her bonds.

'Because…' He looked into her simmering olive gaze, knowing that if he was demanding the truth from her then the least he could do was return the favour. 'Because despite what your father decreed, I used to fantasise about you. Not consciously, *never consciously*. But in my dreams…that was different. And…'

This bit was the hard part. The bit he'd never admitted to before, not even to himself. 'I guess I'd always wondered… hoped, maybe…that you might have done the same.'

Stella's heart ticked away madly like a thousand halyards tinkling in a stiff breeze. There'd been a vibe between them as teenagers—not spoken about or acted upon. But if she'd known that he used to dream about her she might have ignored her father's silent censure.

He looked so serious kneeling between her legs. Torn, surprised even, as if his words had come as a revelation to him too.

How could she not reciprocate?

Her father was gone and, even if he hadn't been, she was an adult, no longer needy of his approval.

'Yes,' she murmured, their gazes locking. 'Lady Mary is me. Beneath all those layers of clothing she has my heart and soul. *And* my desires.'

The admission was amazingly cathartic. She licked her lips, her mouth suddenly as dry as the ties binding her to the bed.

'When Vasco stormed into my head, I knew he was you. Deep down anyway—it took me a little while to recognise it consciously. And when I knew that, I knew whoever his woman was going to be, she would be me.'

Rick smiled triumphantly as Vasco had done at Mary's capitulation.

Stella rolled her eyes. 'I fantasised constantly about you when I was a teenager. And when I was writing the book…'

She stopped and blushed at the memory. 'Let's just say that Mr Buzzy got quite the working out.'

Rick blinked, relief flooding through his veins. 'So, I wasn't alone?' he murmured.

She shook her head. 'You weren't alone.'

Rick laid both hands over his heart and mouthed, 'Thank you.' Then he leaned forward and brushed his mouth lightly over hers, murmuring, 'Thank you, thank you,' as he dropped a string of tiny kisses before sitting back on his haunches again.

She quirked an eyebrow at him, a smile on her face. 'You going to untie me now?'

Rick shook his head as he ripped at the Velcro fastener on his boardies, a wicked glint in his eyes. 'I'm just getting started.'

The next day Stella and Rick were at six metres and just about to head back to the boat for lunch when Stella spotted a large shape looming below them. Visibility was still excellent but the find was partially obscured by a cascading wall of coral. Rick's breathing and heart rate picked up and he made a conscious effort to control them as they headed down to explore further.

As they neared, the ghostly grey shape of a remarkably intact, large, old wooden ship appeared. It was wedged into some kind of rocky ravine, the outer ledge of which fell away into the deep blue abyss of Pacific Ocean.

They both hovered above it for a moment, their torches aimed at the broken waterlogged beauty, stunned to be finally staring at something they'd both wondered from time to time ever really existed.

Was it *The Mermaid*? They couldn't know for certain—yet. But Rick felt sure in his gut—either that or it was Nathan's presence. They glided slowly through the waters surrounding the ship, trying to find any outward identifying marks but, whatever the origins, Rick already knew from years of salvage experience they had found something truly amazing.

They circled it in awed silence, the coral encrusted ship spooky in its watery grave. Adrenaline buzzed through Rick's veins as he became more certain, the dimensions of the find putting it in *The Mermaid*'s league. They didn't attempt to go in—that would come later when a more detailed survey had been undertaken. Too many divers had got themselves trapped and died in wrecks to be foolhardy.

And, as Nathan had always drilled into him, a shipwreck was a sacred site. The final resting place of the poor souls that had perished along with it and as such was to be treated with respect.

They discovered a figurehead when the bow came into view but it was too decayed and encrusted with weedy growths and coral life to tell if it was the laughing mermaid that had famously spearheaded Inigo Alvarez's ship. The nameplate proclaiming the ship as *La Sirena* was nowhere in sight.

Of course. It was never that easy...

Rick and Stella made their way to where the ghostly shape had settled on rock. He shone his torch, inspecting the damage, trying to ascertain a point of impact. Stella shone hers too, the beam hitting rock, a flash of something reflecting back. Stella looked closer, her heart thumping loudly in the eerie underwater stillness, her hand reaching for the object. She scooped it up, lay it flat in the palm of her hand, shone her torch on it.

A gold coin.

Rick felt a tug on his leg. He turned to find Stella, who was grinning like a loon, holding up what appeared to be a round coin. His heartbeat climbed off the scale as she passed it over.

It was gold and in good nick. Gold coins of good purity usually survived in water unscathed, unlike bronze coins that were degraded by salinity.

It was also Spanish.

It still didn't confirm the ship was *The Mermaid*. Archae-ologists were going to have to decide that. But it was another strong indicator.

He grinned back and hugged her tight.

A couple of hours later they were back on board and had fin-ished notifying the necessary people. Rick had organised for the marine archaeology company they used to send a team and had started the application process for a permit to salvage.

Stella was on deck looking at the marker buoy in the dis-tance when Rick came up behind her. She was in a vest top and sarong and he pressed the chilled bottle of champagne they'd brought way back in Cairns for just this occasion against one shoulder as he kissed the other.

Stella jumped at the shock of it, then turned in his arms, and hugged him. 'Thank you,' she whispered.

Rick held her close, the boat bobbing gently. Realising Nathan's dream had meant as much to her as it had to him.

'I've been thinking,' she said, pulling back slightly. 'When they confirm it's *The Mermaid*, I'd like to bring Dad's ashes out here and scatter them.'

Nathan had always wanted them scattered at sea, but until now Stella hadn't felt ready to let him go.

Rick nodded. 'Good idea.' He smiled. 'Let's drink to Nathan,' he said.

They eased apart and he handed her the flutes as he worked the cork. Its pop was lost in the vast ocean surrounds and he quickly filled the glasses, handing her one.

'To Dad,' she said, holding her glass aloft.

Rick nodded, clinking his flute against hers. 'To Nathan.'

He glanced at her as she sipped the frothy nectar and she grinned at him. The breeze caught her drying blonde hair and the sun sparkled on the sea behind her like the champagne bubbles. She looked like a mermaid, a *sirena*, and he felt deep, deep-down-in-his-bones happy.

'What?' Stella asked as the glitter in his gaze became spec-
ulative.

'I think I love you,' he murmured.

The words fell from his lips and he didn't even bother to
recall them because he knew in that instant that they were the
truth. He did love her.

He'd loved her for ever.

Stella blinked. 'Okay…no more champagne for you,' she
joked.

He laughed, then sobered, his gaze roaming her lovely familiar face. 'I'm sorry, I know that's sudden but…it's not really. It's just been a long time coming.'

Stella realised he was serious. Her pulse tripped. 'But…I
thought the ocean, this…' she threw her arm out, indicating
the glory of the scenery around them '…is your great love.'

Rick shook his head. 'This is nothing without you.'

Stella's heart clanged like a gong. She didn't know what to
say. The fact that she loved him too was a no-brainer. It was
suddenly as clear as the tropical waters fringing the pristine
Micronesian reefs. In fact, she couldn't remember a time she
hadn't loved him. It had always been there, snuggled inside
her. She just hadn't been free to admit it.

Until now.

But she'd already lived through one broken marriage because of the sea and, no matter how much she loved him, she
couldn't be with a man who wouldn't put her first.

Stella shook her head sadly, not allowing her love to bloom.
'It's not enough, Rick. Love's not enough. My father loved
my mother, after all. I need to know you want me more than
the ocean. That you'll put me before it. Something my father
and your father *never* did.'

Rick stood firm, understanding her reticence, knowing that
what he did for a job was hard on relationships but refusing
to be cowed by it. 'You want me to walk away, I'll walk away.'

Stella lifted her hand and stroked his whiskers. 'I can't

ask you to do that, Rick. I'm not going to forbid you from the ocean—I saw how much grief that caused my mother in the long run. That has to be your choice.'

Rick lifted his hand to cover hers with his. 'The sea is not an easy mistress, Stel. She's selfish and addictive. But I've seen what happened with Nathan and Linda, and lived with the consequences of my father's inability to choose between two loves. Believe me, I know the heartache of that just as well as you and I don't want that for you and me. Rest assured, Stel, I will never put the sea before you.' His hands slid to her shoulders. *'Never.'*

Stella wanted to believe him. His brilliant blue eyes glittered with openness and honesty and she wanted to fall into them for ever. But… 'So tell me how this works?'

He shrugged. 'Up until we decide to start a family—'

'Wait,' she interrupted, the boat suddenly rolling under her feet a little. 'We're starting a family?'

'Sure…one day. Absolutely.' He frowned. 'I thought you wanted kids?'

Stella felt a lump in her throat as she nodded. 'Absolutely. Not soon. But one day.'

'Well, until then,' he continued, gently rubbing his hands up and down her arms, 'we can divide our time between Cornwall and salvage jobs. You have a portable career, Stel, and you love the business as much as I do so…why not?'

Why not indeed? Stella thought. Just because her parents hadn't been able to compromise didn't mean that they couldn't. And he was right—as long as she had a laptop and access to the Internet, her office could be anywhere.

'And when kids come along I'll manage the business from land and get someone in to do the hands-on stuff.'

Stella frowned at him. 'You would do that?'

He nodded. 'For you, I'd do it happily. I guess I'd like to go and spend the odd few days here and there at sea, checking on things, and when the kids get older we can take them on the *Persephone* in the school holidays just like when we were young.'

Stella felt that lump thicken as he painted a picture she'd dreamt about all her life. One that she was supposed to have lived with her own parents, but her father hadn't ever been able to stay on land long enough.

'How do I know you're not just telling me stuff I want to hear?' she asked. 'How many times do you think Dad promised Mum things would be different next time he came home?'

Rick pulled her in close to him. 'I'm not Nathan.'

He held her fiercely for a moment before pulling back to look into her eyes.

'I loved your father, he was like a father to me, you know that, but I was a little jealous of you having Linda. I wished she could have been my mother too. I never got how Nathan had such a terrific woman like Linda and didn't appreciate her. I've seen two male role models in my life blow it with women who loved them with far-reaching consequences, so, trust me, I won't ever make that mistake.'

Stella nodded. She believed him when he said he didn't want to make the same mistakes. Hindsight had put them both on the same page and love would keep them there.

'I love you,' she murmured, freeing her heart, letting her love bloom.

Rick smiled a slow steady smile as she said the three words he'd been waiting to hear nearly all his life.

Better late than never.

'Is that a yes?' he asked.

Stella laughed. 'A yes to what?'

'Embarking on a lifelong pleasure hunt?' he teased.

She smiled and raised her glass. 'That's a *hell yes*.'

Rick lowered his head. 'Then let's get started,' he whispered.

* * * * *

#3117 IN THE HEAT OF THE SPOTLIGHT
The Bryants: Powerful & Proud
Kate Hewitt
Ambitious tycoon Luke Bryant's power and passion will lay scandalous Aurelie bare.... She's determined not to let him get beneath her skin, but faced with the sexiest man she's ever met, Aurelie can't resist just one touch!

#3118 NO MORE SWEET SURRENDER
Scandal in the Spotlight
Caitlin Crews
Ivan Korovin's only solution to a PR nightmare created by outspoken Miranda Sweet is to give the ravenous public what they want—to see these two enemies become lovers! But soon the mutually beneficial charade becomes too hot to handle!

#3119 PRIDE AFTER HER FALL
Lucy Ellis
Lorelai is an heiress on the edge, hiding her desperation behind her glossy blond hair and even brighter smile. Legendary racing driver Nash Blue never could resist a challenge—and he begins his biggest yet: unwrapping the real Lorelai St James....

#3120 LIVING THE CHARADE
Michelle Conder
When buttoned-up Miller Jacob needs to find a fake boyfriend, Valentino Ventura, maverick of the racing world, is the last person she wants. Up for the job, Valentino can't wait to help Miller let her hair—and whatever else she wants—down!

You can find more information on upcoming Harlequin® titles, free excerpts and more at www.Harlequin.com.

EXPHPCNM0113RB

REQUEST YOUR FREE BOOKS!

2 FREE NOVELS PLUS
2 FREE GIFTS!

PASSION GUARANTEED SEDUCTION

YES! Please send me 2 FREE Harlequin Presents® novels and my 2 FREE gifts (gifts are worth about $10). After receiving them, if I don't wish to receive any more books, I can return the shipping statement marked "cancel." If I don't cancel, I will receive 6 brand-new novels every month and be billed just $4.30 per book in the U.S. or $4.99 per book in Canada. That's a saving of at least 14% off the cover price! It's quite a bargain! Shipping and handling is just 50¢ per book in the U.S. and 75¢ per book in Canada.* I understand that accepting the 2 free books and gifts places me under no obligation to buy anything. I can always return a shipment and cancel at any time. Even if I never buy another book, the two free books and gifts are mine to keep forever.

106/306 HDN FERQ

Name	(PLEASE PRINT)	
Address		Apt. #
City	State/Prov.	Zip/Postal Code

Signature (if under 18, a parent or guardian must sign)

Mail to the **Reader Service:**
IN U.S.A.: P.O. Box 1867, Buffalo, NY 14240-1867
IN CANADA: P.O. Box 609, Fort Erie, Ontario L2A 5X3

Not valid for current subscribers to Harlequin Presents books.

**Are you a current subscriber to Harlequin Presents books
and want to receive the larger-print edition?
Call 1-800-873-8635 or visit www.ReaderService.com.**

* Terms and prices subject to change without notice. Prices do not include applicable taxes. Sales tax applicable in N.Y. Canadian residents will be charged applicable taxes. Offer not valid in Quebec. This offer is limited to one order per household. All orders subject to credit approval. Credit or debit balances in a customer's account(s) may be offset by any other outstanding balance owed by or to the customer. Please allow 4 to 6 weeks for delivery. Offer available while quantities last.

Your Privacy—The Reader Service is committed to protecting your privacy. Our Privacy Policy is available online at www.ReaderService.com or upon request from the Reader Service.

We make a portion of our mailing list available to reputable third parties that offer products we believe may interest you. If you prefer that we not exchange your name with third parties, or if you wish to clarify or modify your communication preferences, please visit us at www.ReaderService.com/consumerchoice or write to us at Reader Service Preference Service, P.O. Box 9062, Buffalo, NY 14269. Include your complete name and address.

Evangeline is surprised when her past lover turns out to be her fiancé's brother. How will she manage the one she loved and the one she has made a deal with?

Follow her path to love January 22, 2013, with

THE ONE THAT GOT AWAY

by Kelly Hunter

"The trouble with memories like ours," he said roughly, "is that you think you've buried them, dealt with them, right up until they reach up and rip out your throat."

Some memories were like that. But not all. Sometimes memories could be finessed into something slightly more palatable.

"Maybe we could try replacing the bad with something a little less intense," she suggested tentatively. "You could try treating me as your future sister-in-law. We could do polite and civil. We could come to like it that way."

"Watching you hang off my brother's arm doesn't make me feel civilized, Evangeline. It makes me want to break things."

Ah.

"Call off the engagement." He wasn't looking at her. And it wasn't a request. "Turn this mess around."

"We need Max's trust fund money."

"I'll cover Max for the money. I'll buy you out."

"What?" Anger slid through her, hot and biting. She could feel her composure slipping away but there was nothing else for it. Not in the face of the hot mess that was Logan. "No," she said as steadily as she could. "No one's buying me out of anything, least of all MEP. That company is *mine,* just as much as it is Max's. I've put six years into it, eighty-hour weeks of blood, sweat, tears and fears into making it the success it is. Prepping it for bigger opportunities, and one of those opportunities is just around the corner. Why on earth would I let you buy me out?"

He meant to use his big body to intimidate her. Closer, and closer still, until the jacket of his suit brushed the silk of her dress, but he didn't touch her, just let the heat build. His lips had that hard sensual curve about them that had haunted her dreams for years. She couldn't stop staring at them.

She needed to stop staring at them.

"You can't be in my life, Lena. Not even on the periphery. I discovered that the hard way ten years ago. So either you leave willingly…or I make you leave."

Find out what Evangeline decides to do by picking up THE ONE THAT GOT AWAY by Kelly Hunter. Available January 22, 2013, wherever Harlequin books are sold.